INFALLIBLE

D1488458

Brian Dillon

Fairmount Hill Publishing

Printed in the United States of America

FAIRMOUNT HILL PUBLISHING
PO Box 2216
Mashpee, MA 02649-2216
(www.fairmounthillpublishing.com)

ISBN 978-1-60643-108-5

A man may lose
his sight yet again regain
a joy in living. He may lose all
that he owns yet battle back to happiness.
Indeed, lose his very life in a just cause yet
one day rejoice in new life. But pity
the man whose integrity is lost for
the happiness he seeks becomes
death itself.

The Ancients

Forever Dedicated
To those who come forward
to speak the Truth.

INFALLIBLE

by

Brian Dillon

THE ANCIENT WOODEN room was a sea of sounds and echoes as sixty-three ten-year-olds readied themselves for another day of school. Coats and hats were doffed and soft little hands emptied books from book bags to place them inside little wooden desks. This day's drill was a tad more trying as water droplets from the morning rain covered the desk tops.

When every child had books secured a nod was delivered to the first student at the first desk. Row by row, like little soldiers, they marched into the narrow cloakroom to stow their belongings — hats, coats, boots and bags.

The return trip was out the rear of the cloakroom, into the lobby and back into the room's main entrance to stand again beside their seats. Nine rows of seven kids got the drill done quickly and efficiently. A nice piece of work.

On her platform, fingering rosary beads, eyeing the big clock's second hand was the original weapon of mass destruction herself, Sister Beatrice Serene. At precisely eight-forty five Sister BS made the sign of the cross. The instant her hands touched the class recited an Our Father, a Hail Mary and the Pledge of Allegiance and the day began anew. Another nice piece of work.

As always, the day began with religion. First a lecture and then, as it had for centuries past, questions from curious young minds.

"And so it is that our Holy Father in Rome is Infallible, he can never be wrong. He is the one and the only person on earth who speaks directly with God Himself. And that is why the Catholic Church is the one true religion."

Never wrong! Imagine. Little minds strained to comprehend what it must be like.

Like a herd of startled zebra, frantically waving little hands shot skyward, each begging to be chosen to ask the next question, hoping for some wisdom from a woman with, dressed head to heel in layers of black wool on a steaming June day. The nun chose an immaculately dressed little girl with a matter of fact delivery.

"My mother wanted me to ask you, Sister. Does our Holy Father in Rome ever get to go to Heaven? Does God fly him up in a special space ship for meetings and if so..."

Virginia O'Day stood and delivered in a manner and tone which demanded the attention of the entire class. Even at the tender age of ten she was controlling and obnoxious. Her father was a big source of money to the church. The family lived in a mansion surrounded by a brick wall, whose gate was always closed. She was delivered to school each day in a huge black Cadillac, emerging crisply dressed, acknowledging the lucky few on her way inside. A nun or two would usher her arrival with smiles of approval as she climbed the steps to make her grand little entrance. Only then would the big car roll away.

A sharp contrast it was to the grandchildren of the great unwashed. Not everyone owned a car in those days, never mind a shiny Cadillac. Her test scores were always top of the heap, homework always perfectly completed. One might have assumed the O'Days had their own in-house professor who saw to such chores. Along with family wealth, and a full pass from the wrath of the nuns, Virginia excited intimidation in anyone who approached her airspace without an invite, much like the glare of a hungry tiger. She was a self-anointed, arrogant little snot who knew well her station in life.

Daydreaming, as it was called in those days, was bad business. Right up there with idolatry, heresy and stiffing the collection box. Penalties ranged from hard glares to promises of eternal damnation.

Seated several rows from little Virginia was the boldest, most impudent little bastard ever to shine a seat at St. Catherine's. He was Michael John Kilgallen and his irreverence for the One True Church, the only valid entrance into the Kingdom of Heaven, knew no bounds. Like a master mimic a timely facial expression poked full of holes two thousand years of sacred lore, all to the delight of anyone who dared watch. A ten-year-old comic genius with wit, timing and perfect delivery.

"The answer to your mother's question, Virginia, is that the Holy Father sees God in ways which we can never begin to understand."

Shielded by the only fat kid in the class Mike turned to his neighbor, jacked open his eyes and mouth, folded his hands in prayer and shot an expression of exquisite relief skyward, as if the reply to

Virginia O'Day's question had just solved the riddle of man's existence in the universe, ending his search for meaning, and unlocking his spiritual shackles to bathe finally in eternal bliss.

Four nearby kids suppressed laughter to the point of near suffocation. Shielded by the fat kid Mike continued his blasphemy, mouthing thanks and praise Heavenward as the class awaited the answer to the question of whether or not the apostles could fly.

As if on cue, a vicious fart. Unholy build-up from one of the laughers no doubt. It turned a couple of heads which made it all the more hilarious. With the poker-faced sanctity of an Archbishop, Mike turned and waved the sign of the cross in the general location of the fart as if bestowing his personal blessings on a well timed effort. With that, the pain of the laughers rocketed to unbearable levels.

Little Maggie Bennett then stood and delivered. "If Jesus is the Son of God, who is God's wife?"

"Margaret, God is a bachelor. He is not married."

Little Freddie Duffy got the nod. "If Charles Atlas can hold up the world could he be related to God?"

"No, Frederick."

With each divine revelation Mike's rapture intensified as did the suppressed laughter of his audience. Surely one would blow a hole in his pants or rupture an organ.

From the mind of Pamela Deegan, "Did Jesus and the Apostles have a truck or a tractor to get around in back then?"

"Indeed not. Donkeys were it in those days but I'm glad to see you wore your thinking cap today, Pamela."

Inevitably the shit would hit the fan and Mike once again would suffer hell on earth. But it was some show, all right. Would the laughers would suffer the local version of eternal flames for participating? This was the trap, the conflict. The show was a sensation but one paid dearly for the ticket. What torture and humiliation would the poor kid endure today? Probably his usual. Each laugher prayed that the nun would wear herself out on Mike alone. After all, it was his show. He produced, directed and had the lead role. All others mere spectators.

Faces the color of ripe tomatoes, peppered that section of the class. But for the moment, the noise of the question and answer period covered the little theatre.

Paul Sullivan wanted answers to the classic James Cagney good guy-bad guy riddle. "If a guy robs a bank and shoots some people and then the cops shoot him but he gets out the back door and runs to the church to confess because he knows he's gonna die but when he gets there he dies on the front steps but he was gonna confess…"

Virginia O'Day looked to her right and held a steely gaze. Among Virginia's unique abilities were bird-dogging for the nun, and being offended by nearly everyone else.

The nun followed her lead, spotting a student whose pink head looked about to pop off its shoulders. Her eyes narrowed and her face hardened as she drew a bead on the fresh-faced little devil who, now bathing in undreamed of levels of rapture, continued his blasphemy of Jesus Christ, the one true Church, the Kingdom of Heaven and all Its earthly agents.

A nearby student wore a look of terror as if a mistaken association with the goings-on of this pagan might warrant his own crucifixion. One took one's life in one's hands when an audience in Mike's little theatre. oblivious, Mike continued his silent mock of Almighty God Himself.

Sister BS had inherited a number of handles over the years. Sister Samurai, Sister Mary Gallows, Sister Mary Trigger Happy, Sister Mary forty-five, Sister Mary Machete. Machete stuck because it had rhythm to it. Sister Mary Machete. It communicated. That became 'the sword'. But, until her last student draws a last breath, she will be remembered simply as 'The Blade.' The Blade was well into her second generation of butchering the minds and scalps of little kids.

The eyes locked, the class silenced, the executioner readied. Like a panther The Blade moved from the platform, a silent and pissed off machine in black robes. Something conjured from a child's nightmare. A horribly alien apparatus of wheels and pulleys powering the form hidden in black. What was now on its way to Mike seemed an illogic, like perfectly working knees which bent in both directions. With compelling intention it rolled up Mike's aisle and was upon him before he could ask the object of his blasphemy for help.

It gripped his hair viciously with both hands and yanked with all its strength, back and forth, side to side. Mike held on to his desk for dear life while the head jerked and muscles wrenched. All the while The Blade's black bulk screamed insanely of irreverence, paganism and the certainty of eternal suffering.

Having endured these rages for years Mike was now little more than the poster boy of stupidity and everlasting damnation among the student body. For nearly a minute the foul smelling blackness railed and wrenched. A girl, seated nearby, began to cry and then wet herself. The class watched as an ignorant mob from a past culture would witness an execution, strangely silent and unblinking, staring morbidly as a head rolled or a body dangled. Mike was then lifted by his hair from his seat and dragged to the platform in front of the class.

"Perhaps," The Blade howled, "you'd like to recite for us your multiplication tables, or name for us the Holy Days of Obligation. Or perhaps the name of our Holy Father in Rome. No! You cannot because, as every one knows, you are stupid and sinful and you will spend eternity with the devil and the damned in the fires of hell. Isn't that true?"

Mike didn't answer right away so The Blade yanked his hair again delivering more pain.

"Well, isn't that true?" The Blade screamed.

"Yes, Sister."

"The note I'm going to give you is to be brought home and signed by both of your parents and delivered to me on Monday. Is that clear?"

"Yes, Sister."

"We'll see if your father can't beat the fear of God into you. Now remove yourself from the rest of us. Get into the cloakroom, out of my sight."

A badly beaten and thoroughly humiliated little boy walked gingerly from the platform and disappeared from view. The Blade nodded victoriously to a sea of faces washed in fear, and one smirking little Virginia O'Day.

Chapter 2

INSIDE THE CLOAKROOM Mike could only stare numbly at the floor. He checked his hair for blood. He sat on his own lunchbox, back to the wall. Looking at the hanging coats and the boots on the floor, he wished desperately that he was someone else, even the fat kid who sat in front of him with the perpetual red cheeks, who never spoke to anyone and had no friends.

As he began his silent cry The Blade raged of the never ending fires of hell to the unblinking innocents. The image of his father's belt was frozen in his mind.

"Inattentiveness leads to disbelief and disbelief to mortal sin. To die in the state of mortal sin is to suffer the agonies of eternal damnation. Hell. Imagine your hands thrust into burning, white hot coals. Imagine the unbearable pain of flesh being seared from your bones, turning to ash before your eyes. Hell is to suffer this torment on very inch of your body for eternity. Burning and burning, minute by minute, for all time."

She swept an arm through the air and turned in Mike's direction. "In that cloakroom is the devil's work, a walking, talking one-way ticket to hell. No other student in this entire school is as inattentive, unprepared, irreverent or sacrilegious. Am I getting through?"

It seemed that she was. Each pair of eyes wore the look of terror.

"Nor has anyone, ever to attend this school, to my knowledge, had worse report cards. I want you all to know."

Mike heard her bitter denunciation, checked his hair for blood again and closed his eyes.

The secret hiding place in his head, where the birds delivered candy bars and the bears took him for rides, where the kind-eyed, infinitely patient old man, with long white beard, who applauded as Mike hit magically appearing baseballs into the hills, was becoming more difficult to reach. Today the kind old man stood perfectly content as the bears romped and the birds chirped. None seemed to miss his presence, as if they too were alerted to his sins, and had cast him out without concern.

He awoke to silence wondering if he'd been abandoned. But the boots and coats were unmoved. Then he heard someone cough.

The Blade spoke, "Your attention, students."

A shuffle of bodies echoed as the children shifted in their seats.

"Father Devlin will be here shortly to congratulate Virginia O'Day and Raymond Fleming for their excellent achievements this marking period. I will ask you both to present yourselves at the front of the class to accept your awards when the time comes. Is that clear?"

"Yes, Sister," the two students said in one voice.

Mike heard the announcement and was envious of the winners. What must it be like to be inspired and

accepted in the real world and not constantly hammered and pounded?

The hours passed slowly. Mike ate his lunch
where he sat, as the class was suffered through
geography. He was counting boots and multiplying by
three when he heard the front door of the school open
and close. Then the slow and labored footfalls of a man
on the steps. His eyes widened in concern and he
moved further to the wall in an effort to camouflage
himself among the boots and coats. The footsteps
stopped outside the cloakroom's rear exit. All was quiet
for a moment. Then, the striking of a match and a loud
intake of breath. Then a voice.

"Some trouble in school, Mike?"

At the sinister tone Mike's little heart stopped.
How was it possible? The priest, with his bushy
eyebrows, bald head, and weird lips. Could God have
called the Pope and the Pope called the priest? Of
course, thick as thieves, all of them connected. Mike
was as guilty as Barabbas and the word went out.

By now his aunts, uncles and cousins would be
gathered at his house, heads hung solemnly, begging
the Saints to spare the soul of the little kid who just
couldn't keep his fucking mouth shut and pay
attention.

"Mike?"

"Yes, Father."

"Some trouble, today?"

"Yes, Father."

"When?"

"During Religion, Father."

The priest took a drag and blew out a volume of smoke and poked his head into the room.

"Come to the sacristy after school. We'll have a talk, you and I."

This was very matter of fact with something else not quite right attached.

"Yes, father."

There would be no dodging the priest, no excuses, no forgetting this conversation had occurred. Mike's ever present concern of returning home to constant shrieking criticism from his mother and a beating at the hands of his father seemed now as desirable as ice cream. That was at least predictable. But this out of the blue invite, to the sacristy of all places, spoken in a menacing whisper, had Mike's imagination running. Was the priest aware of Mike's blasphemy? This question only raised more questions. Or... could he be witnessing the mercy of Christ at work for the first time in his life? Was he to be imbued with new abilities far beyond those of mere mortals, where wandering attention and shitty report cards mattered not?

But why the sacristy? He wasn't even an altar boy. He was dumb and damned yet the questions persisted. Why me? Why not a smart kid? Why the sacristy? Why this private audience? Was he, Mike Kilgallen, the chosen one? After all his pain and suffering had the world come to its senses recognizing in him qualities found only in the Saints? Was the priest to announce this to him privately by way of a small ceremony? Had 'someone' somewhere above the clouds decided to include Mike on their roster? Would the nuns gather and kneel before him on Monday?

Why was his stomach in knots? These hopeful imaginings, he realized, were as half baked as the idea of his favorite human being, Willie Mays, appearing at his back door, wide eyed and smiling, on a Saturday morning beckoning him to the field to play ball. Hope of anything positive faded at the recollection of the priest's voice, not unlike Boris Karloff's in 'The Mummy'.

From the cloakroom he endured the ceremony as best he could. The Blade announced the winners, Father Steven Devlin, priest, Pastor of St. Catherine's Parish, protector of the flock, handed out award plaques, and the class applauded the winners. The priest delivered a few words on the virtues of hard work, homework and paying attention. He added that these years at St. Catherine's would pass swiftly and would one day be remembered as the finest years of their lives. The lessons learned here, by the Sisters of Charity, would one day guide them into the Kingdom of Heaven.

The priest acknowledged the winners once again, blessed the class, bid the Blade a pleasant afternoon and walked from the room.

The weekend wasn't looking good. The note loomed large. That could screw up his baseball plans. What lay ahead was anybody's guess. By two o'clock he'd figured out how to calculate the square footage of the cloakroom floor.

The walk from school to the sacristy was not filled with the usual curiosity of a child. Not today. He stretched the five minute walk from school to the church into twenty, all the while regretting his earlier antics. He'd become darkly concerned of the consequences. More so this afternoon than usual, because of his earlier dialogue with the priest. Usually, after a beating in school, the gloomy trek homeward in the afternoon was saddled with the anxiety ridden mystery of whether or not his mother knew. If that was the case then there'd be trouble. During Christmas vacation there was a surprise phone call from the Blade, and it wasn't pretty.

This day was different, however. There was a strange new level to his anxiety. There was no wonderment in spotting rabbits and other wildlife, no desire to search the bubbling brook for turtles or frogs. No desire to throw rocks or dam a stream or even to play baseball. The closer he got to the church the deeper his foreboding. If a herd of buffalo trampled by, or Robin Hood himself and his band of merry men were seen on horseback among the bushes and trees it would not have mattered an iota. Such was young Mike's concern.

Chapter 3

"TAKE OFF ALL of your clothes and bring to me your underpants."

In that moment everything changed. For one blinding instant he was certain the voice was trustworthy and forgiving, and that being naked in the sacristy was just a formality that every kid went through. That perhaps this ritual was sort of like taking a leak. It came so naturally you just didn't talk about it. Nevertheless, he found himself bouncing from the mental wall of the terrible present to the wall of where he desperately wanted to be. His legs began to shake. He was a lost little boy pitted against gigantic forces. No good guys in white hats with gleaming guns would storm the sacristy and carry him to safety. No Hoppy, no Gene, no Cisco Kid would appear in the nick of time to save his soul. Not today.

The priest was seated in an armchair near the door so escape was impossible. For an instant Mike thought of taking a stand, picking up the gold candle-holder to his left and bashing in the ugly balding head. Instinctively he knew this to be just, yet he was damned if he did and damned if he didn't. It all made the predictable world of his perpetually pissed off parents look like life with Roy and Dale.

Instead he took the turn to hell and began to un-
dress. He apologized to the wise old man of his secret
hiding place and said goodbye. His actions this day, he
knew, forever preventing his return.

He stood in only his underpants turning sideways
as he took them off to hide his privates from the priest.
In his nakedness he became aware of some invisible
quality within himself evaporating like dew in the
morning sun. Get it over and done with he decided.

"Bring them to me this instant."

Mike obeyed, keeping as much distance as possible between himself and the priest. There he stood
naked and vulnerable.

"Now walk to the corner and kneel in prayer with
your naked bum to me."

He couldn't recall that in his catechism. Of course
he couldn't recall much of anything in his catechism
but he'd bet his baseball glove no such lesson existed.

What if some kid from school appeared? Just
popped his head in the door. What then?

*"What's up? Come on in, take your clothes off, re-
lax, say a few prayers."*

Willie Mays wouldn't approve. He doubted it'd be
a popular topic at the field on Saturday.

*"Hey Mike, how come you didn't show for the
game after school?"* a friend might inquire. *"Me? Why, I
was praying bare ass with Father D. Who won? Get any
hits?"*

"Oh, ho ho ho – oh, ho ho ho" the priest moaned.
This wasn't any sacrament Mike had heard of. Ever.

No, sir. He'd received his first Holy Communion,
attended two weddings and a couple of baptisms, but
everybody wore clothes. Milkmen, mailmen, bus drivers

and clumsy little infielders popped into his head and he longed to be out among them, with his clothes on, feeling normal. He felt the heavy eyes of the priest on his rear end. He wondered what on earth was happening but dared not move a muscle.

A framed print leaned against the wall in front of him. It held the image of a young peasant boy under a halo staring serenely skyward. In the reflection he could see the priest wearing his underpants on his head, like the bathing caps the old ladies wore at the beach.

Holy shit! The priest was unzipping his pants. Then he started doing something with his thing. Quick rapid up and down strokes. Mike prayed for all he was worth. He called to Jesus for the very first time, as a soldier in battle would pray for his life.

The priest rose from the chair with his thing showing. He began talking like a girl reminding Mike of his aunt Harriet, who never shut up and was forever looking at herself in the tiny mirror she pulled from her purse.

"This is so unlike me. Whatever will the neighbors say?" He then put on a pair of high-heeled shoes, and with his hands on his hips began sashaying side to side. From his briefcase he took a blonde wig and put it on over Mike's underpants, threw a long silk vestment over his shoulders, placed hands on hips again and rested on one leg. Then he lifted a foot.

"Michael Kilgallen, you incorrigible little pile, I want you to know I purchased these with the money collected from last Sunday's donations. They're a tad tight but they screamed to me, 'take us home, take us home'. So I bought them. Had to have them. Oh, aren't they stunning? No, they're not Buster Browns you little imbecile. They're from Paris. All the rage. I think the Archbishop will adore them, don't you?"

Mike didn't answer.

"Well, don't you?"

"Yes, father," said Mike. Then the priest's voice changed to snarling command.

"Come to me you bare-ass little whore," he said.

Mike stood on shaking legs, standing in such a way as to hide his privates and salvage any remaining dignity.

"I said come to me."

Mike moved his little naked body to the priest.

When at arm's length the priest squatted so their eyes met. He moved Mike's arms to his hips and stared as if Mike was a side of beef.

"It's the will of God, you understand. My mother's hair was long and blonde and beautiful."

The priest then touched Mike's privates. His skin crawled. The sensation, a grim and dark degradation forever to be kept secret. The mother of all traps, the secret.

"Tell this tale and you will burn in hell. And sooner than you think. I shall see to it personally. Do you understand?"

Mike smelled the fowl breath.

"Yes, father," he said shaking.

The priest kissed him from his lips to his knees and groped his rear end. It went on a good long time.

Chapter 4

THE WALK HOME was a dreamy underwater effort. He was filthy, violated and he smelled of the priest. His rear end hurt from the penetration. He was miles below shedding tears, a universe removed from his innocence. A good deal of what he'd left home with that morning did not arrive with him in the evening. Oddly his regret of not striking the priest with the candle-holder persisted. He hurt from his hair to his heels and the day's instructions by the one true religion and its earthy minions was not over yet.

His father's car was in the driveway, a real bad sign. He reckoned he was very late and began to construct a false account of the missing hours. His mother, whose high scratchy whine would fray the nerves of a fresh corpse, would demand to know his whereabouts and his father would be in a murderous rage. There'd be no mercy from them.

He walked through the front door to the usual din of radio, television and screaming sisters. A butt dangled from his mother lips as she cleared the dinner table. Her head was in rollers. As one of his sisters watched the television another abruptly changed the channel and a scuffle ensued. Even the puppets on the screen were fighting.

His mother spotted him. "Ya late!! Where the hell you been? We ate already. Your father's out looking for you and there's gonna be trouble. What the hell do you think this is? What the hell have I brought into this world? Whaaaat?"

The ranting continued as she carried dirty dishes into the kitchen. Mike's defense against the never ending static was to lie. It wasn't really lying, he thought. It was replacing his trench warfare lifestyle with a more peaceful setting, uncluttered with resentment, noise and punishment.

"Well? Where the hell were you?" she screamed from the kitchen.

"Over at a kid's house helping him put his trains together."

"What kid? Do we know him? Is he Catholic?" The baby began to cry. "Now look what you've done. Your father is going to absolutely kill you and I'll tell you right now, you have it coming to you." The tone of the voice a mix of screeching animal, subway brakes and siren.

He had a decision to make. Show his crazy mother the note this second. It might even quiet her down, but it might not and his father was due back any second. All he'd need was to see her screaming head in rollers and he'd start swinging. She'd hand him the note with some cynical remark, *"Look what the little genius has brought home to us this time."* An automatic ten lashes.

Mike was computing the methods and motives of two crazy people, three counting the Blade. Forget the sacristy shit. His first concern was remaining healthy enough to play baseball the next morning. So despite his maniac mother, fighting sisters, crying baby, fear of his father walking through the door, and the humiliating events of the day he carried on his delicate analysis. All of which was a little like predicting the weather in the North Atlantic.

There had to be a solution. Breaking the news of the note would combine all the latest upsets into one beating and that'd be that. Something to consider. A long shot was his aunt Harriet appearing with a bag of booze. They drank like thirsty Arabs whenever she showed. He willed her old green Chevy to the front of the house. A little much to hope for but it was Friday after all. All this scheming to squeeze in a little baseball with his buddies.

A mind good in working order could rightly conclude that simple solutions, clearly available to most, were unavailable to Mike. His mental machinery jammed when certain facts collided. On one hand there was his gift for making kids laugh, love of baseball, Super Man, cowboys and playing games in the woods with his friends. All of these things he enjoyed immensely. On the other hand, nothing he enjoyed won him any popularity with grownups. Every move he made just seemed to piss them off.

School and home, a form of hell in themselves, were constant concerns and bad for his health. Absolutely intolerable, all of it a waste of damn good baseball time. He'd long ago tired of asking the Almighty for a break. It seemed those who should be buying the salvation pitch weren't concerned at all; pissed off grown-ups, the Blade and now the biggest square peg of all, the priest. His time, he figured, would be better spent praying for them, not himself. Them and their quest for the afterlife.

Besides, who'd want to spend 'all time' with them? Eternity at High Mass? Fuck that. And where was heaven? Who made the rules, and what kind of second baseman would that guy make? Probably some clown who'd botch every ground ball that came his way. Could baseball itself be a mortal sin? If that was the case then every kid in the country would burn, watch horrified as the flesh of their throwing arms bubbled and boiled and turned to ash before their eyes. Over and over, forever. It seemed grownups were happy as hell about going to hell. None of it made a lick of sense.

Unanswered questions, to the curious, behave as a magnetic field would behave. Anything from anywhere at anytime gets sucked in to satisfy the 'hunger' for an answer, so starved is the person for the truth. Wrong answers, sideways answers, up side down and inside out answers serve splendidly. And it all passes for normal.

Mike's reasoning powers were being taxed from constant reminders in school and at home that all things pleasurable were sinful, to be avoided. Chocolate cake and root beer, farting with your friends, laughing in school, might have hell itself as a final reward, with no baseball, no cowboy shows, no cartoons tolerated. Just a big, fat, sweaty, bare-ass bully with a whip in his hand and horns on his head ordering you to shovel coal into a giant furnace.

How was it so many grown ups could violate what was constantly beaten into him? Everywhere were sad, sorrowful and pissed off faces. For the life of him he couldn't figure why suffering was the way to go, why everything fun was sinful. Was he hell bound by way of the electric chair, as an uncle once remarked to his father one fine day upon seeing Mike's report card.

Nevertheless the very thought of cracking a book, his only salvation, produced within him inexplicable pains. His bag of books may as well have been a box of scorpions. Little by little Mike was disappearing into his own wild-wild west and his own planet Krypton, very gradually inheriting 'the guilt'. Still he'd not formulated a plan to get out of the house and onto the field the next morning.

The front door opened with a crash. His father's eyes narrowed and blazed fire.

"Come here, you."

Mike walked in fear to his father who grabbed his shirt collar and yanked.

"Listen to me stupid, I just spent the last half hour of my life looking for you. Where were you? I come home, and no stupid. Where's stupid? I say to myself. He must be out getting even more stupid than he was yesterday, if that's possible."

Mrs. K appeared, shaking her head in disgust. She placed a bottle of beer in her husband's hand and he took a long swallow. He then gritted his teeth. He placed the bottle on a table, took off his belt, gripped it and ripped it viciously across Mike's back.

"You miss supper again and I'll wear myself out on you. Are you hearing this or am I talking to myself?"

Mike laughed aloud at his thought that his father was indeed talking to himself, as usual. So he got a second reminder of who was in charge.

"Hey stupid, you getting a big kick out of this shit or something? Well?"

"No" said Mike.

"You be here when your mother feeds the family. You think I got nothing better to do than walk the streets looking for a moron. I take it up the ass all week long to put food on the god damn table so you can eat it. I have to go looking for you again and I'll wale you good."

Mike's mental rebuttal was, *'You know what, ass-hole. I go to school, put on a decent show, get some laughs, get my ass kicked. Go to church, get screwed. Come home to get reminded how thick in the head I am. So fuck y...'*

The squeal of brakes from the street was music to his ears. His father looked out the window, tone changing for the better.

"Fuckin' beautiful," he said under his breath. "Hey, Claire, you're sister's here with a big bag of sauce." He cleaned off a chair. "Must be Friday," he said happily. "Get outa here, you," he said to Mike,

Harriet had arrived and the first miracle of the weekend had occurred. The next bunch would happen tomorrow on the crude baseball diamond to play the greatest game ever invented.

Chapter 5

THE SKY WAS blue and the air was warm. The dew on the dirt and sparse green grass sparkled. Birds sang morning melodies and pulled breakfast from the ground, a ground now muddied by rain but all was right with the world.

Shortly the field would be trampled from the motions of little feet into something resembling a flat plane. For now, though, ground balls would be interrupted by earth's imperfections but that was okay. This rough diamond was like no other parcel on earth to a ten year old. He had no deed yet he owned it, he couldn't take it with him but it was his, it was even okay if others owned it too. All were invited. All were welcome, any shape, any size, batless, gloveless, no matter. Show up, know the rules, keep your eye on the ball, that was it. There was a game to play. There was action, competition, admiration, victory, others the same reality, someone to sit with and talk to, no one to slap you around or threaten your soul. Black was black and white was white. The universe was a diamond. It was warm and the sun was out.

High tinny voices chattered like birdsong cheering the swing of the bat, the throw in from left, the short peg to first, the strike call, grounders up the middle, needless slides into second, close calls at home, the arguments, the score. No decent human would argue that life was close to perfection on the field of play. And it was warm and the sun was out.

First base was a rock, second was a stick, third was the tree, and home a hole in the ground. By noon a whole bunch of baseball had been played. No one really knew the score, only that personnel had to be switched because one side got clobbered all morning long and kids were falling asleep at their positions from boredom.

At the bottom of the umteenth Mike yelled from the old log which served as a dugout. "That's it. Joey, you gotta switch sides and Kenny and Denis can only bat lefty."

"That's not fair," countered Denis.

"You've got six homeruns facrisake, Denis."

"So do you."

"Yeah, but we're on the same side. It's about fifty to two. Those guys need some muscle at the plate or we bat blindfolded. Besides I'm getting hungry. What time is it?"

"Me too. It's lunchtime," somebody said

"Okay. Let's go eat. See ya this afta. Kenny, bring Bells back. We need men in the outfield. And get his glove, too, will ya?"

That was a command by Mike that all would be back for an afternoon session and his promise that the competition would be crisply balanced.

Bells, whose real name was Albert, was Kenny's brother. Bells could really play. But just after last season, when baseball turned to football Albert had gone deep and run smack-dab into third base. Third was the tree. In the fall it served as part of the side line for the football field and the kids dropped jackets, hats and gloves to extend that side line making a workable gridiron. Every article of clothing was also a first down marker.

Albert was running as fast as his little legs would carry him for a pass Mike himself had thrown. He met the tree full steam and was out cold before he hit the ground. So kids being kids, immensely interested in someone who was actually knocked out and laying before them and not seeing any blood or deformed facial features, didn't think anything too serious had occurred. But after a minute Albert still wasn't moving and his brother Kenny started to cry and the other kids began to panic.

Mike didn't know what to do either but instinctively began yelling as loudly as he could in Albert's face. "Albert! Albert! Can you hear me? Al, come back, will ya. Albert."

Then all the other kids joined in the shouting for Albert to return to them and to full consciousness. It worked and in a few seconds his eyes moved. Soon Albert was moaning and blinking and talking nonsense, to the huge relief of his brother. Within minutes he was on his feet wobbling around the side lines. A couple of kids began to toss the ball around. The crisis had passed and they were antsy to begin play again. Denis held up two fingers and asked Albert what he saw. Albert only said 'Bells' and everyone started to laugh and the name stuck.

Bells wasn't involved in anything more violent than checkers these days. Mike had stopped by his house a few days after the collision just to say hi. His mother was really nice. She opened the door with a genuine smile and invited Mike inside and escorted him to Bells' room. Bells was reading a dinosaur book. He seemed okay, no slower or faster than he was before the collision but still not a hundred percent. Mike asked Bells what he was reading and Bells showed him the pictures of ferocious beasts eating each other. Bells began to name them and the periods of time they came from. There was all kinds of books and science shit around the room and some pictures of old planes on the wall. The room was neat and clean despite all the stuff around. Bells even had his own radio.

Then Bells' mother knocked softly and brought in cookies and milk. The house was peaceful and calm with no threat of someone crashing through the door to devour you whole. Mike sensed a tranquility he'd never imagined. No noise, no apprehension.

He was struck with envy, of Bells sitting comfortably with a book in front of him and reading it. He was probably the smartest kids in his school who inhaled everything he read. He wanted to be friends with Bells but he was sure Bells would sooner or later discover he was the stupidest kid in his school and how often they beat him up and too many people knew that already.

He thought Bells could care less if he ever saw a football again. He'd come up with some very impressive plays in the huddle and had gotten by Mike a few times when they were on opposing sides. Nobody got by Mike. So Mike felt sadness that Bells might not be seen at the field anymore. Bells could really play and Mike liked that in anybody. He ran across Bells a few times during the winter and they said hi to each other.

It's okay if you're winning but after a while if the game goes lopsided you feel like losing just so things get interesting again. Things would change after lunch, he promised the losers.

"Whose gonna be on your side Mike?" one of the losing players asked.

"Don't know yet. Don't worry. Okay?"

The kids who got clobbered left the field slowly with hanging heads. The winners, jogged away heckling the losers. In a minute the field was deserted, everyone on his way home for lunch. Mike wondered what lunch at Kenny's house would be like.

When all the kids were gone Mike took to the woods and walked among the bushes and trees until he could see his house. His father's car was in the driveway so lunch at his house was out. That ran the risk of getting smacked around. So fuck that.

He walked the half mile or so to his grandfather's. That was always good for a bowl of soup and a sand-wich. And kind words.

His grandfather lived alone. His grandmother died when Mike was six. A stroke they called it. Mike couldn't quite get his wits around 'stroke'. A lot of old folks got it. His idea of it was a lightening bolt that came inside the house and zapped you while you watched TV. The two times Mike had gone to a funeral, his grand-mother's and old Mr. Metzgar's up the street, both had died of a stroke.

One day Mike had helped Mrs. Metzgar drag out her trash and was invited in for a snack. And there was old Mr. Metzgar, glued to the TV with a blanket on his lap, so Mike concluded that lightening really could come indoors even when the sun was out. But it only happened to old people so kids were off the hook.

Maybe one would sizzle the priest or The Blade one day soon. The thought of the priest gave him the creeps. Today was Saturday and confession was at four. He wondered about that. Suddenly the day was not as bright.

Mike opened the screen door and went inside. The kitchen was as neat as a pin. From the window he spotted his grandfather in his usual warm weather pose, bent over in the garden. He checked the frig for food. There were always surprises like jello and ice cream and stuff. He looked again out the kitchen window and went to join his grandfather.

"Hi, Pop," said Mike.

From under a thatch of white hair the old man turned and smiled. "Why, Mike what brings you here on such a grand day as this? No baseball this marnin'?" he checked his watch.

"Yeah, we played. This afta, too."

"Well now, I'd say it's toim for a boit a' lunch. Would ya be joinin' me then, Mike?"

The Irish brogue and warm greetings were always a great comfort.

The old man struggled to his feet. "Oh boyo, Mikey. Some advice for ya', niver getold. Arr ya hoongry? I've a lovely pea soup tatoiyv been savin' for just the right guest. And Mrs. Mac dropped by with some Irish bread, so we'll be havin' tat as well, with a little jam and buthr."

He waited a moment for his back to straighten. There were rows of this and that coming out of the ground but nothing yet mature enough to pick. When things came popping out there'd be plenty to eat, making the late winter and spring look like a famine.

During the lean cold months his mother would send him on the half mile 'leftovers' trek to her father's. Mike always volunteered for the duty just to get out of the house, no matter the cold.

In the spring all his grandfather's friends from the old country would congregate at someone's house for something or other; pull rocks out of the ground, repair fences, sharpen lawnmowers, move appliances, pull storm windows. One Saturday morning Mike walked over with a bag of leftovers. There was a truck in the driveway.

Jim Carty, Pop's friend from the old country, had volunteered to move some old lady from a third floor walk up in Dorchester to a nursing home, far away. Jim was a great big tall guy so all the tough stuff came his way. Mike had gone along for the ride, seated between the two old guys listening to them blab the brogue about this and that.

It was lots of fun and he helped load the little stuff. Up and down the steps he ran to the dismay of the two old guys. After a nonstop hour of that he was asked nicely by his grandfather to sit still for awhile. Jim didn't look too happy. They were sweating, breathing heavily, had slowed to a snails pace, and were still a long way from being done. They became concerned it would take two trips.

It took most of the afternoon just to load the truck and by the end of the job the old guys were mighty pissed off about the whole deal because they still had to drive somewhere and unload it. So rather than make two trips they loaded the truck until it resembled something out of a Porky Pig cartoon.

At the top of the pile was a bureau minus its drawers, tied down securely. Or so they thought.

Now it was off to the next stop but first, lunch, a great relief to Mike. They went to Dwyer's Tavern, parked, locked the truck and went inside, taking a table next to a window so they had a view of the goods.

"Don't want'ny villains marching off with tat now, do we?" said Jim, sitting very heavily.

"My God, Tom, who on earth'll get us up out of these chairs?" he snickered.

A smiling waiter in a white apron approached. He had thick black curly hair and big ears.

"Gentlemen," he said in a soft brogue.

"Two Guinness and a coke, wouldja, Danny. And three stews," Jim said.

They sat a silent minute, the old men adjusting to their seats.

"Not a word of this place to your mum or we're both of us in trouble. Your word on that?" said Pop.

Mike nodded enthusiastically.

Big Jim winked and nodded without a smile, as if being here was indeed secret business. The waiter arrived with drinks. Mike felt part of a club for the first time. He had a shared secret to keep and he would. Both Guinnesses were raised in a silent toast. They waited for Mike to raise his and he did, with both hands.

"What a beauty Annie was, Tom," said Jim looking out at the pile in the truck. "Brings tears to me eyes. Losing her da and her husband in 'The Uprising' like she did. Niver the same after that. Niver."

Mike listened to his grandfather's explanation.

"We're talking of the lovely woman owns them few things, Mikey," he nodded at the truck. "We knew her when she wasn't much older than you are now. Back in

Ireland. One of them beauties made you talk over yourself. You'll know soon enough. Am I right, Jimmy?"

Jim nodded and swallowed. "Couldn't keep me eyes to meself. Black hair, green eyes, and them..." he held his hands out.

"Nor meself, when she was nearby," said Pop.

To Mike he said, "There was bad times in Ireland when we were lads before your mum was born even, and poor Annie there" nodding again at the truck, "lost them she loved most to it."

"Niver the same again," added Jim.

Mike drank deeply from the sing song poetic Irish chatter of the two old men. It seemed his new best friends had lived a thousand years. He was about to ask them if they knew Robin Hood when the stew arrived.

The truck was overloaded to say the least and the ride was loud and bumpy. Every nut and bolt seemed to be undoing itself. Jim rolled slowly through the narrow three-decker Dorchester streets until they were at last on a highway and the ride smoothed. Then he drove like they'd just robbed a bank. For a while all was fine when suddenly there was an odd shift of weight.

"Jazuzanmary Tom, what was tat?" he looked from mirror to mirror. "I can't see a bloody ting."

The wind had gathered in the drawerless bureau that topped off the pile that was poor Annie O'Toole's life. Like an enormous balloon it flew side to side, held only by the rope that Jim himself had fastened. Jim had wound the rope only through the thin wooden drawer separators. Now the damn thing was a parachute threatening to lift men, boy and truck off the road and into the Blue Hills. For a moment the bureau was so high in the air that both side mirrors were useless.

"What tahell's gonon back dere, Tom?"

Both white heads were bobbing frantically up and down trying to glimpse something in their side mirrors. Mike had turned, kneeling backward in his seat, to get a view out the back window, through all the shit in the truck. He could barely see that traffic had slowed to a crawl. But big Jim rolled along in fearful oblivion. Suddenly the truck lurched forward as if released from an enormous grip.

"Chroist above, Tom. I tink we've lost the bloody ting. Jazuz! How am I to answer for tat, now?"

The rope had snapped and now the bureau was no more than a physics specimen, a twisting spiraling brown blur, travelling through space at sixty miles per hour twenty feet above the road. It hit with an explosion and disappeared into a rolling cloud of dust.

"Jazuz, did ya see that? Was it the bloody..."

"Twas, Jimmy."

"Should we stop?"

"To sweep Annie's bureau into a tidy pile of dust? Get off the bloody road, willya, before we're pinched."

Five minutes later they were in another tavern with a fist full of Guinness.

Jim suddenly laughed aloud. "By God, Tom," he raised his glass, "at least Annie's drawers are safe witus, now."

Tom laughed heartily as well. "An' surely they are, Jimmy. Safe witus now, are Annie's drawers."

Mike could only smile at the two laughing men.

Mike mopped up the last of his pea soup with Irish bread, thick with butter and jam. He was stuffed to the gills, happy as could be over lunch with Pop.

"Well Mikey, you look as full as a boot, arya?"

"Yup."

"Ask your mum if you can't come over Friday. I'll fry up steaks and we'll watch the fights on the telly. Then we'll have a surprise for desert, you and I."

"Okay," said a wide-eyed Mike. "I got kids waiting at the field, Pop. Baseball." With that Mike was on his way.

Tom hadn't heard squat from his daughter, or that husband of hers, about the bureau or the bar rooms. No news was good news where they were concerned. So he figured his grandson was the sort to handle trust and keep his word, something the world sorely lacked.

He was concerned for the boy. If he could survive his own parents, if he survived them and the Church he'd rule the world. He knew well, mostly from the old days, that craziness was as contagious as a virus.

He watched Mike run down the driveway, up the street and out of sight. How he loved the boy.

If Tom O'Bannion had known of the priest he'd have killed him slowly on the altar of his own church that day. Crushed out the unholy perverted life between his two powerful fists under the gaze of Christ and the Holy Mother Herself.

And big Jim Carty would've held Tom's hat.

Chapter 6

AT THE FIELD the kids were gathered in a bored bunch under the shade of third base. When Mike appeared they stood to greet him. From a distance he knew something was not right. All that remained were Kenny, Joey, Denis and two eight year olds.

"Gary Latch is in the woods beating up Bells. All the other kids went home," said Joey.

Mike's eyes opened wide in fear and hate.

Gary was the bully from the other side of the woods. He was scrawny with pimples, a big-mouth who intimidated little kids. He couldn't run, hit or catch anything. He was pale, clumsy and slow. But he was fourteen and much bigger than Mike.

"Is he alone?" asked Mike.

"No, his brother's with him," said Kenny, near tears.

"How long they been in there?"

"A little while."

Word was, Gary's brother had been to reform school during the winter which only added to the moment's fear and hopelessness. The kids at the field had christened him 'Creature from the Black Lagoon'. Then just 'Creature'.

Mike knew well the Latch's reputation. They were older and bigger and they smoked. The summer before, Gary and Creature, and two other thugs had walked in and taken bat, ball and gloves from the little kids, occupying the entire field for an hour. In engineer boots, dungarees and weird haircuts with cigarette packs rolled into tee shirt sleeves, they played ball among themselves.

Mike was unimpressed as he watched the unco-ordinated motions, slack muscle and slow gait of all four bullies. He even taunted Gary to his face knowing he could outrun them all if he had to. But during the occupation one of his friends got smacked in the face. A smack, Mike knew, which was intended for him, and in retaliation for his taunts. The kids could do nothing but wish away the bullies. When they were done the bullies threw all the kid's equipment into the stream at the edge of the woods.

On the ground beside one of the gloves was a sling shot. Mike picked it up and pulled the rubber sling.

"Bells'?" asked Mike.

Kenny nodded.

"Get rocks. Shitloads."

The kids jumped into action. Shortly there was a neat pile of rocks. Nobody said a word but all knew they were up against something brand new and terrifying.

"Fill your pockets. I'm going in the long way. You guys go in until you see Gary. No further. And be quiet. Wait'll I hit one of them. When I yell, charge and start throwing."

"Are you kiddin' Mike? They'll kill us," said Joey.

"Then stay here and guard our fucking shit, Joey. Okay?"

They all knew there was no one and nothing to guard the shit from.

"Awright, I'm going too."

Mike and his crew of tiny assassins then set off into the woods for battle.

Saturday afternoon was confession and that included every Catholic under the sun. Sins by the ton were told and forgiven on Saturday. Everything from pissing in the woods, to throwing rocks at cars, to feeling your big sisters' tits, to bank robbery, was washed away. Gone. Like it never happened. It was a bloody miracle how easily the gravest offense was forgiven and what a soft touch the Almighty really was.

Facrisake, you couldn't get a fucking seat on Saturday sometimes. Go in, fess up, say a good Act of Contrition, do the penance, which was no more than a couple of quick prayers, and go out and do it all over again. Who in his right mind wouldn't cough up a buck a week for that kind of protection? Yes indeed, it was a beautiful thing.

Unless you were unafraid of thought. Which brought up questions. Serious questions. But like a politician's promises those questions were given short shrift on Sunday. Spoken in monotone half-truths were sermons laced with glib and paper thin assurances that this way, was the only way. If you believed, had faith.

All answers for the afterlife were available on Sunday but not a single one for the here and now. Faith was Sunday's commodity and half the world got in line to load up.

The young nun nervously made her way through the curtain into the compartment and knelt without making a sound. This was the confessional in the convent's chapel. A priest from one of the nearby parishes was given the duty each week to hear the sins of the sisters.

From the adjacent compartment she heard the passionate mumbling of the current penitent. Her palms began to sweat. On her inquisitive mind this early afternoon were not necessarily the issues which weighed upon her sense of what was right and what was wrong. What weighed most in her thoughts, what consumed most of her calm nature this day was just one question, and how that might be answered by her confessor. Neither spiritual struggle nor prayer had supplied one, by way of Divine Inspiration or otherwise. Her love of life and her devotion to mankind bestowed upon her an aura that was the envy of most. And the ire of a few.

She was taller than the others and thin. Her hair was red and her features sharp. The calm and humble eyes burned with intelligence. She was utterly devoted to her calling. She acted with an assurance of God's Blessings and of her chosen path. Teaching the young. She'd have gone to the ends of the earth to teach the children. It had meaning enough to entertain, at times, hopes of a blissful reward. When she weakened, overcome by such greed, she noted them as something to confess.

She was one to search daily and deeply for correct interpretations of Church dogma and Almighty God's unwritten messages. Her name was Sister Tess and she was stunningly beautiful inside and out. The adjacent wooden lattice door slid closed with a thump and the priest rolled her way in his confessional box. It was her turn at the plate.

Bells was being held to the ground by Gary. The ugly Gary sat atop Bells pinning his arms as Creature spit and dropped dirt onto Bells' face. There was some chatter but Mike couldn't make it out. There were lots of trees and bushes between him and the enemy camp. Bells was crying, that's all he knew.

He took the sling shot from his back pocket. Bells had put together a fine piece of work. Mike placed a stone in the webbing and took a practice shot. It's power and accuracy had mildly frightened him. He was as nervous as could be. His mouth was dry and his legs were shaking and he hoped to God he was up to the task.

The imminent charge into the enemy camp made his breathing quick and uneasy. He reminded himself he was physically superior to the uglies in that he could come within a few feet of them and still make a clean getaway. Fist fighting was out of the question. That would surely be a losing proposition. If captured he'd be tortured. That ran the risk of losing Bells, the rest of his men, and his real estate if it came to that. The uglies would terrorize them all summer long.

He wasn't panicking but that was no comfort and did nothing to ease the shakes. This mission and all of his hopes for a pleasant summer had one chance and one chance only for success. Surprise and immediate shocking pain from direct hits into soft spots in the enemy.

But first he had to stop himself from shaking. He listed the advantages. He possessed a superior weapon, the element of surprise, a squad of men, and a lot of other shit, too, now that he thought about it. Instantly clarity of thought presented itself. He became aware of the rightness of the mission and without any emotion whatsoever, he observed the uglies. There they were, only yards away. There was no hate rising within him or even disgust. There was only the mission, rid the territory of distraction.

He piled his rocks in front of him and picked six of the best ones. What the fuck, he didn't need fifty rocks. Wouldn't have time for them. He'd win or lose it all with six or less. But the first one had better find its mark. He locked and loaded and stood up. Then he began his march to destiny.

With her eyes tightly shut she whispered so that the question traveled only a foot. "Is it a mortal sin, Father, for a servant of God to want a child of her own?" "I'm so full of happiness at the thought of it yet so committed to my life here that I felt a need to inquire..."

There appeared a minute breach in the communication. An abrupt but silent termination. Then the perception was upon her. Regret of choosing this question, this day. She heard a rustle of garments and opened her eyes. To her horror the box was empty. Her nervous system began to overload. The curtain flew open and there stood Father Devlin, beams from his evil purposes impaling Sister Tess to the very spot where she knelt.

"You whore to the devil," he yelled. "Get out of here, get out of this sacred place and take your wicked thoughts with you. You dare contaminate the rest of us. Leave this house of God this very minute."

She was frozen on her knees and could not move.

The priest's volume doubled. "Leave I tell you."

In rare form he was, bellowing fire and brimstone the likes of which had never been seen or heard. Echoes resounded thunderously, the eyes of the other penitents opened in disbelief and fear.

The terrified Sister Tess scrambled out of the compartment on hands and knees, past the feet of her accuser and up the aisle to the back of the little chapel. Humiliated beyond words, scarred for the remainder of her earthly existence, she righted herself and ran out the door.

The Blade smiled and nodded her satisfaction in the direction of the priest.

Never engage in combat until all possible advantages have been secured. And never engage an enemy you know you cannot defeat. Mike had analyzed all of this and a dozen more details. Even the cowardice of his own men. But he was certain of this, the ugly brothers were cowards themselves. A couple of clean hits would scatter them and even if they retaliated during the summer Mike could counter and eventually win overall.

He was within range and he was loaded for bear. He stepped out of the shrubs, took dead aim at Creature and fired. It struck him in the cheek.

"Ow, Jesus. Whathefugwasthat? Oh my fugingod, I'm bleedin," he shrieked in shock.

Mike reloaded and yelled at the top of his lungs. "Hey, Gary." He marched further into the clearing, fired and hit Gary in the back. Gary was off Bells in a flash, his skinny arms flailing behind his back to pull out the arrow he was certain was stuck there. Creature went for a rock and was hit in the shoulder by Mike's next shot.

Then the troops made their move and the screaming started. Kenny ran up to Creature, pegged a rock with all his might and caught him with a direct hit on the head. The rock bounced off Creature's head into the bushes and Kenny let out a war cry. Joey, pegging rocks like a mad man, was laughing so hard at how far the rock had bounced off Creature's head, and Kenny's

Jekyll & Hyde transformation into lunatic screamer with murderous intentions, that he couldn't yell or see straight for a while. The two eight year olds were back a ways but at least they were pegging rocks in the right direction. Strength in numbers.

Mike regretted his decision of only six rocks but the enemy was toppling and there was plenty of ammo underfoot. The ugly brothers began to panic. The cries from Creature and Gary were loud and guttural. Like the guys who got tossed off the big log in 'King Kong'.

Denis caught Creature with a perfect sidearm peg in the back of the leg. Then another to the neck which landed with a wicked sounding thwap. The ugly brothers were going down. Bells tripped the retreating Gary and kicked him hard in the face. Blood was flowing, the assassins smelled it and the intensity increased. Revenge today was indeed a wonder drug. It was fucking beautiful.

"Hey fuckstick! Coming back tomorrow? This one's going right up your asshole," yelled Joey, who seemed to have grown a foot in the last minute and couldn't wipe the smile from his face.

Gary caught one on the knee cap, the bully cried out and hobbled backward, mouth and eyes open wide in shock. The uglies were hit again and again until they were crying and screaming for mercy while desperately clawing their way to safety. But no mercy came their way. Rocks from the slingshot hissed through the air with deadly accuracy. Mike was hitting flesh with every attempt. The good guys were marching forward, gaining ground with every step, raining rocks on the ugly brothers.

Then all of a sudden, like a telepathic command, the firing ceased. The uglies were now far enough away and beaten badly enough to call it quits. The victorious group stood silent, the reality of their huge win not quite set in their heads. They watched the uglies disappear into the greenery.

Then they went to Bells to check him out. He seemed no worse for the wear. A few good welts to the neck and head, some bumps, some embarrassment and a dirty face but that was about it. The warriors gathered around as he shook dirt from his face and hair. His look was one of apology for being dumb enough to get captured.

"Couldn't have made it happen without this, Bells. This thing is fuckin' wicked." Mike launched a rock at warp speed into the woods.

"Mike?" said Bells in a tone of stunned admiration, "that was fucking unbelievable. I think they woulda killed me. They said they were gonna. Creature had a knife."

"Not anymore," said Joey. "This one?" he held up a seven inch blade. "You want it, Mike?"

"Throw it off the bridge on your way to school, Joey. If you want, okay? Here's your slingshot, Bells."

"Thanks. You can keep it, Mike." Bells then sighed heavily. "I know you guys saved my life today but could you guys do me a favor? Could you guys call me Albert, please. My mother's getting pissed off about the Bells thing. Now I got to explain this to her."

All nodded and just like that Bells was no more. He was Albert again.

The eight year olds just stood silent, admiring the real live warriors. Mike was their hero and they just wanted to stay in the woods with him all day. He called all the shots, beat the bullies and won the day. He was like George Washington or something.

Denis spoke. "Look at all the blood. Do you think they'll die?"

"Who fucking cares. Yeah, fuck them," interjected the two eight year olds. They looked at each other oddly.

Joey laughed. "Who saw the rock bounce off Creature's head? Kenny hit him with a wicked perfect shot and it bounced off his fuckin' head like it was a tennis ball. Honest to God, it was pissa."

"Fuckin' pissa shot, Kenny," added Denis.

The adrenaline was going home and the kids walked into the bushes to take leaks.

"I think some of the rocks I fired mighta stuck in Creature. This thing is pissa. It's wicked fuckin' accurate," said Mike.

"They're inside his fucking head, Mike," offered Joey.

"He's got rocks in his head," added Denis.

They were all pissing in the bushes and laughing. Then Joey said, "We'll call him Rocky. I baptize thee Rocky in the name of father, and of the son, and of the holy slingshot."

Then as they were still pissing Mike said, "Hey, I got a great idea."

"What?" they all said. And he ripped a wicked loud fart. Then Denis farted.

"Gas bombs. Women and children first," laughed Kenny.

"Now I gotta take a wicked shit," said Joey and worked his way further into the woods while laughing his balls off. They all stood around, stuck in the glee of laughter.

Mike said, "I don't feel like playing this afta. Let's go down the Square and get some ice cream. I got fifty cents. You guys got any money?" They emptied their pockets and made a pile of silver.

"Hey, Joey, you got any money?"

"Wait a sec," yelled Joey from far away.

They counted again, and searched their pockets again.

Joey yelled out. "Hey, you guys. Come here, you gotta see this."

They made their way over. When they got there Joey was nowhere to be seen but they heard him laughing.

"Where are ya? Hey! Joey! Where the fuck is he?"

"Look out be-lowwwww!!" they heard him yell.

Thirty feet in the air, squatting on a limb taking a shit was our man Joey. At the sight of shit falling from the sky, there was a volume of laughter.

"Holy shit," somebody said, and the laughter of the six tripled at the double meaning. Everybody was laughing their balls off.

It only got better when Mike pointed up and said with a big smile, "That asshole's one of my best friends."

"That asshole lives on my street," Denis added.

From one of the eight year olds, "God, there's a ton of it." The other said, "It's raining shit."

Then Joey yelled, "Hey, anybody down there got the sports page?"

That got 'em going again. Mike, armed with the slingshot, faked a shot at Joey's ass, creeped up on the shit like it was a rattlesnake, and fired into it.

"Hey", yelled Joey, "leave my shit alone."

That did it. They all fell to the ground.

On the ground once again, the grinning Joey said, "There's no fuckin' door on that bathroom?"

"There's no fuckin' floor either," laughed Denis.

Then Mike put his hands on his hips, frowned and pointed to the shit, "Hey, which one of you little bastards left his shit here?" More laughs. "Well, whose shit is it?"

Then Albert went deadpan and pointed to it. "Who needs this shit?"

The two eight year olds were laughing their asses off. "It's Creature's brains," said one.

"Shit for brains," said the other.

Then a free for all of, "Cut the shit. What a pile of shit. Can you believe this shit? Are you shitting me? What kind of shit is this? Where does he come up with this shit?" That went on until they were weak from laughter.

Denis said, "Hey Bells, sorry, I mean Albert, after we get ice cream we'll walk you home okay, and tell your mother it was a wicked head first slide into second that drove in the winner, and that's what fucked your face up. Okay everybody?"

Everybody nodded. They headed down the Square for ice cream.

"I just hope your mother doesn't give you any shit," somebody said. They all laughed.

No game of baseball would top the day's excitement. They owned the day and it would be one of those priceless nights in the life of a boy, laying in bed reliving adventure and huge victories with his friends, listening to the chorus of insects and night noises outside his window, until his eyes finally fluttered shut in the wee hours and he drifted into a deep sleep.

Chapter 7

MIKE WAS DOING just that on Sunday morning, sleeping deeply, when suddenly he was yanked from his slumber and thrown to the floor of his room while his father screamed blue Jesus at him. In his hand he waved the Blade's note.

"When were you gonna show me this? In July, you little idiot? You get dressed and you get your ass to church. And I'd do some praying if I were you. Then you get back here and you wait for me down cellar. You understand that? Or am I talking to myself again?"

Mike got a back hander on the side of his head to start the day. He was dragged from the room and down the stairs to the breakfast table, where his mother smoked a butt and read the paper. The high pitched whine began.

"Where the hell did we get you? What kind of idiots do you think we are? Why do you continually torment us the way you do? What have we done to deserve this? How does it feel to be so stupid?"

With that she got up and tossed some cold oatmeal into a bowl and dropped it in front of Mike.

"You're gonna need this, you little dope."

The baby began crying.

"Cha-rist Almighty! Look what you started al---ready!"

Morning everybody.

The walk to church wasn't long enough. Well, the note wasn't a problem anymore, that was for sure. He couldn't shake the cold dread of seeing the priest on the altar. If that was the case he'd have to skip communion. Keeping the priest at a safe distance was becoming a full time occupation.

To Mike's great relief Father McAuley was on the altar. Thank God. Now he could fall in, march up and receive the body and blood of Christ as if he deserved it, proof he'd confessed everything the previous day, that he'd suffered terribly and was sorry for his sins.

Latin. Everything was in Latin. How did everyone know it so easily? Was he really as thick as they thought he was? He took a gander for a positive sign, a bright set of eyes, a knowing smile, a nod, a wink, a reassuring "don't worry kid, you'll get it." But nothing. Everyone just knew it, that's all.

Mike received communion without having confessed the previous week's offences of swearing his ass off, shitting in the woods, breaking windows in the old house after church with Joey, and forcing his youngest sister to smell the finger he'd stuck up his ass. "PEEEUUUUU", she'd said in disgust and ran off crying. He caught her and gave her fifteen cents before she reached her father.

He had to receive. He couldn't be seen skipping communion. For all he knew his father might be there spying on him. If it got back to him, that meant a tribunal. He'd witch hunt for mortal sins and Mike would have to invent a bunch to maybe avoid getting smacked around, so... he began his manipulation of time and space to invent yesterday's confession. That could spare him a couple of lashes, which very well might be on the afternoon's agenda. Can't have them showing in school.

Even if he'd gone to confession he wouldn't have mentioned the attempted murder of the ugly brothers and half the other shit he did which would have added up to a Bad Confession, a sin in itself.

So, let's see, if he didn't go at all he'd actually have one sin less, no Bad Confession. That worked. For half a minute. Receiving communion in a state of mortal sin was a maybe. He still wasn't sure what was sinful and what wasn't. Maybe he could make up shit he didn't do and tell that next time. He'd spend the whole week feeling guilty about shit he hadn't even done. Somehow that seemed logical. For a while things were perfectly balanced. But he started thinking again because nothing was resolving.

Hey, wait a sec, he could prob... nah. What if... nah. Could he... nope not that. Maybe... nah. Hey, what about? Fuck it. Adding, subtracting and camouflaging sins was putting him to sleep. He promised himself he'd sort it all out later. What a crap shoot. They had you coming and going. So, what if God could read your mind? So what, fine. Let Him have a ball. And if Mike walked out in one piece... well, just so he could run and his throwing arm worked. He wondered where Willie was playing today.

After mass Mike spotted Joey. He was with his cousin Davey on the front steps. Davey was in Mike's class and so knew of Mike's reputation. Mike felt the anxiety of being found out. If Davey spotted Mike he might tell Joey how stupid Mike was and how often he got beat up by the nuns. That threat faded when Davey went his own way. Mike caught up to Joey and brushed him with his shoulder as boys do. Affectionate displays of strength.

"Let's go break some windows," he said. Joey's eyes lit up in happy surprise.

"Oh, God, Mike. I can't stop laughing. I didn't even tell anybody yet. I went to the field to see the blood again. It's still there. We beat the shit out of them."

"Oh God, that was unbelievable. When you guys charged in like wild Indians I knew we'd kill 'em. You see Kenny? Crazy Horse with rocks. He kicked the shit out of Creature."

"Mike, I laughed all night last night. I laughed myself to sleep."

They walked the long way from church, along the nearly two mile stretch of wealthy homes. The homes which sat back a hundred yards from the street, shaded by tall oaks, whose driveways ran long and circular, the hedges higher and prettier, and the lawns greener.

The old abandoned house was on the other side of the woods which bordered the field on the first base side. There was no rush to be anywhere. It was Sunday morning, they were reliving the glory and enjoying each other's company the morning after battle.

Chapter 8

THERE WAS HARDLY any glass left but they worked on their accuracy anyway. The rocks that got through echoed eerily from within. The house kind of gave you the creeps. The gray paint had faded and flaked. Inside the tattered curtains hung like dead and rotting vines. The arched front door resembled a mouth agape in agony, the two windows above, its eyes, the ones below, its tears.

Mike got the feeling that it was once a happy place but something bad had happened, a long time ago. Now, a useless and forlorn structure deprived of purpose, without life or laughter. Even in the brightness of day it seemed a hopeless, apathetic soul waiting for the last light of its life to expire, pleading for the boys to stop the torment, to go away and to leave it alone. Mike apologized silently and they soon tired of pegging rocks and walked on.

They were getting close to Joey's house. People were mowing lawns and putzing around their yards. The welcome vibration of summer was upon them. Shortly they came upon one of Joey's neighbors who was struggling to get his mower started, one of those old exposed blade jobs. He yanked and yanked but no go. Mr. Cooper was about sixty, bald, and the belt to his pants was up around his nipples. Mike thought how comically shaped Mr. Cooper was, like a Tootsie-Pop, noticing also that his brown pants were as shiny as a new nickel. Below his belt a perfectly round stomach went all the way to the top of his legs, and the fly to his pants, as long as the one on Mike's winter coat, ran the entire length. It was incredible. And he wore a tie like he'd just come back from church. He rested with both hands on his hips and looked at the machine. He was shaking his head slightly just as Joey said hello.

"Well hello there, Joe. And hello to you, young fella," he said cheerfully. "This the damndest thing you ever saw? It was going a minute ago. Did the whole back yard. And just like that she quit," he said through heavy breaths. "Let's try the damn thing again."

He pulled a few times and nothing. Sweat appeared under his armpits, which were only a couple of inches above his belt. "Now that's just the damndest thing, I tell ya."

"Want me to try, Mr. Cooper?" asked Joey.

"Well, why not Joe. Doesn't seem to do a damn thing I tell it, and besides," he pulled a hanky from his back pocket and wiped all the way from his eyebrows to the back of his neck, "two heads are better than one, I always say. Am I right or wrong?"

Mike was reminded of a cartoon character with a perpetual grin. No matter the weather or whatever life dished out, the chubby little fellow was always smiling. He got the idea that life inside Mr. Cooper's house was pleasant and Mrs. Cooper was probably real nice too.

Joey tried a few times with no success. Mike bent to feel the sharp blade.

"Watch yourself down there, young man. Just had 'em sharpened. Had a fella come up from the Square to do it. Damndest thing. Damndest thing. Shoulda done the front first I guess."

Mike undid the gas cap and eye balled it. "Mr. Cooper, you're out of gas."

Mr. Cooper's eyes widened in surprise and relief. "You don't say. Is that a fact?" He peeked in himself. "Well, that's foolishness. Just plain foolishness on my part. Might've worn myself out pulling that damn thing. If that don't beat all. That the damndest thing? Out of gas. I'll be. I want to thank you two young fellas. Mighty kind, mighty kind of you. Hold on, you two. Let's see if Mrs. Cooper has a couple of Cokes for you. Won't be a minute."

In a minute he was back with two ice cold bottles of Coke. "There you go fellas."

"Thanks a lot Mr. Cooper. So long, Mr. Cooper," they said and walked on.

Nearing Joey's they heard the motor come to life and turned to see Mr. Cooper happily back at it. Mike put a foot on a car bumper, pulled his pants up to his chest and made a fat face.

"Wasn't that just the damndest thing you ever saw, young fella. I swallowed a basketball and now I can't get my pants off. Just plain foolishness on my part. Am I right or wrong, young fella?"

Joey laughed a good one.

"I have to go to my grandmother's for dinner. So I can't play today," said Joey.

"Okay. Well, I guess I'll see ya round. Hey, when do you guys get out of school?"

"I think in four more weeks. When do you?"

"Two weeks. I can hardly wait."

Then Joey got kind of serious. "Do kids who go to public school go to hell?"

"What do you mean?" asked Mike.

"Kenny's in my class and he says that his cousin said that if you don't go to Catholic school you go to hell. Jews, Protestants, anybody who's not in Catholic school goes. Even other Catholics."

Mike must have drifted off to Box Canyon during that lecture. Now he was saddled with a brand new dilemma. He hated his school. He wanted to go to public school because the kids looked different. They acted different. He couldn't put his finger on it but he imagined that the teachers, the kids and their parents were like characters on a TV show where everyone got good report cards and nobody beat the shit out of you. On the other hand, public school was evidently a straight shot to hell. This news, hot off Joey's press.

"I don't know," was all he said to Joey.

"Well, could we go for fighting with Gary and Creature or something? Later, when we die?"

"But they would've killed us," said Mike defensively.

"Well, let's say we killed Gary yesterday and then got run over by a steam roller down the Square, we could be in hell right now. Right?"

"Maybe, but I'm not positive. Taking a shit in the woods might be a mortal sin, too," said Mike.

"You tell it in confession?" asked Joey.

"That what?"

"That you took a shit in the woods."

"No. I never do. Besides, where do you think the Indians went?"

"You didn't tell?"

"No. I was gonna but then I kinda didn't think it was a sin, so… Besides I would've had to go all the way home and it woulda screwed up the game so I just went in the woods. Besides, my father was home. Besides, how can killing Gary and taking a shit in the woods both be mortal sins? How can you go to hell for both? It's not fair."

Then Joey said, "I heard if you lie to your mother and father you can go. If you don't do homework you can go. And if you don't tell all your sins in confession you can go. Even if you have too much fun you can go. That's what I heard."

If that was the case, Mike was fucked. At the mention of homework and hell in the same sentence the color in his face drained a bit.

"You can go for all kinds of stuff but I don't know what they are. I think we find out next year," he said.

"Oh," was all Joey could manage.

Neither could see the logic that murder and crapping in the woods were both deserving of damnation. They'd talked themselves up the dead end street of pure theoretical nonsense.

Mike waved a sign of the cross. "Just make a good Act of Contrition and say a couple of Hail Mary's."

He put his foot back on the bumper and made another fat face, "And think twice the next time about taking a shit out of a tree. Damn it, taking a shit in a tree is just plain foolishness. Am I right or wrong, young fella?"

They said they'd see each other at the field. Mike waddled away with his pants still up to his chest leaving Joey laughing.

Walking by the empty field, nearing home, he wrestled with what constituted mortal sin. He walked across the diamond and into the woods to the scene of the battle hoping his spirits would lift. They didn't so he took a leak and left.

His head was spinning with what was sinful and what was not, and who could see inside his head and who couldn't. He wondered how pissed off his father was at the moment and if his mother was nagging. How could hell be any worse than life with those two? At least he wasn't on fire. Yet.

He gazed about his surroundings and imagined he was a young Indian brave. There were deer in the forest and beaver in the streams and screeching hawks far above, and he was on his way home to a cheerful and welcoming wigwam.

As he rounded the corner in deep thought he saw the black car. His whole body shook involuntarily. Parked in front of his house was the priests' car. He knew it from church and the many visits the priest had made to the school. He dashed behind a bush and lay on the ground for a better view. He waited and waited and could not imagine what the priest was doing there.

Reasons ricocheted around his head. A student award was out of the question. Maybe they were going to demote him. That happened once to a kid. Marty McGuire was yanked out around Christmas one year and put back a whole grade. But Marty was practically a mental case. We're talking real slow when we mention Marty. The note was also a maybe, but that was out of the bag, old news. Besides, what connection would the priest have with the note? Unless! Oh Jesus!

Maybe The Blade was with him. That'd be a death sentence. His father would beat him in to meatballs.

Nuns never saw the light of day, though. They were strictly indoor people. Right? Strictly indoor people. Especially on Sundays. They prayed their asses off on Sundays. There were poor people in the Philippines and Guatemala and Timbuktu that needed prayers. Tons of places needed prayers, and the nuns had the duty on Sundays. No fucking way would those two be at his house today. No sir, this was something far more sinister.

He waited for nearly an hour, eyeballing his house. In the dirt he watched bugs he'd never seen. He picked his nose a lot and a bird landed on a branch and hopped around for a while not a foot from his face. He dozed and almost went to sleep but caught himself.

Then, without warning, the priest walked out of the house, got into his car and drove away. Mike watched until the car was a speck in the distance before he budged. Then it hit him. Maybe someone was sick or had an accident. He bee-lined it to the house, his stomach in knots.

He made his way in soundlessly. All was quiet on the home front. Nothing in the air, no static at all. No TV noise, no screaming, no nothing, not a peep. In fact his fear of getting the shit whipped out of him had vanished. But where was everybody? Then he heard the patter of little feet from upstairs.

His six year old sister came down the steps, saw him, smiled and yelled, "He's hewe." Then she said smiling, "A pwiest was hewe. Hewe in our houth. Fava Devil."

Fava Devil? You must be dicking me, and not a soul on earth to share the irony. Fava Devil.

From his little sister's smiling face he knew that somehow it might not be a bad day. But what was up? His father made his way happily downstairs.

"I told Mike Fava Devil was hewe," she said.

He laughed, "It's pronounced Dev--lin, sweetie. Father Devlin. Mike, follow me, I wanna talk to you. You hungry?"

"Ahm, no."

What's all this? thought Mike.

"Ya sure?"

"Yeah." He was starved but he couldn't take his father's sweet 'n kind another second. They went into the kitchen and sat. This was weird and Mike was nervous.

"Oh. Here," his father handed him the Blade's note, signed.

Holy shit. Could dear old dad have tumbled down the stairs and jarred his marbles so loose that they all rolled back into their proper holes?

He checked his father's head for haloes. Stuff like this happened all the time on the other side of the world. Blind people all of a sudden could see, kids walking for the first time, dead people coming back to life.

Something weird was going on. The priest had just left. Mike doubted any miracles had occurred during the visit. But whatever it was, you could bet your ass there'd be a twist.

His mother descended the stairs cheerfully, holding the baby, with no hysterics preceding her arrival. She entered the kitchen, dolled up and smiling. Twist number one.

"Did you tell him?" she asked.

"Nope, I was waiting for you."

No matter the mood in the house at the moment Mike would get the shitty end of the stick. Somehow, some way, as sure as the sun rose in the east.

His smiling mother spoke. "Do you know a priest was in this house not ten minutes ago? A priest, in our home."

His father spoke. "That's right. Father Devlin was here. In our house. In this very room. He came to see you but we told him you were at mass. He just left. He could've walked right into you."

Though well aware of this, his jaw opened wider and wider.

"He said," then Mrs. K quivered, placed her hands over her heart and gazed saint-like at the ceiling, "Well, he said all kinds of things about you. That you were very bright, have a mountain of potential. More than anyone he's ever seen. It's just mis, misapp, misplaced."

"Misdirected," said Mr. K.

"Misdirected, riiiiight. Oh my God. Anyway, he was here for what, an hour, two hours?

"About that. Yeah."

"I can't believe it. I cannot be--lieve what I'm about to say." Then she paused and shook her head slowly, "He said you would, oh my gawwwdddd!!!" She shrieked. "He said you would one day become a priest."

Twist number two, with more on the way.

His father smiled proudly. "Can you imagine how we felt? Can you imagine how we felt at that moment? Honey, get me a beer will ya."

Mike blinked once, stopped breathing and stared at the sugar bowl.

A grinning Mrs. K marched over to the fridge and yanked out a beer.

"He told us that when he was a kid in school in Ohio... in Ohio, Right?"

"Omaha," said Mr. K.

"O-ma-ha, right. That when he was a kid he had terrible grades in school and was destined for a life of crime and that one day a Saint appeared in his..."

Mr. K cut in. "No, no. The voice of St. Peter spoke to him. As plain as day he said."

Mrs. K stood corrected. "Rrrriiiight, right. And it said, no, it told him to go and become an altar boy. And he did. And he got great marks in school from that day on, and then he went to college and after that he became a priest. And he's been all over the world. Can you imagine what goes on in that man's mind? How he thinks?" Then she screeched "This is good news. What's the matter?"

"Nothing," said Mike.

Then his father said, "He says you remind him of him, as a kid. There's no doubt about it."

His mother shrieked again, "Dear God, when he said that, I al---most died. I'm serious. I nearly died."

Mr. K drained the last of his beer, "We're going to the eleven thirty. Right after mass we're going into the sacristy for a tour of how kids learn to be altar boys."

Twist number fucking three.

Mike contemplated the sugar bowl.

"Altar boy lessons? In the sacristy? You gotta know Latin. I could never learn Latin," he heard himself say. He'd never even passed English. Not once.

Mrs. K spoke, "He said it was all Greek to him, too. But he got through it. With the help of St. Peter. That's what he said."

Mike wondered if St. Peter ever stuck his finger up his ass and made his little sisters smell it.

Usually he could think his way out of touchy situations fairly easily, but this one was like a sprained ankle. There was no quick fix, and it'd take some time to get his balance back.

"Well, we're gonna be late." The others marched toward the front door.

Then his father turned kind of hard. "Listen to me. I signed that note 'cause Father Devlin said it would smooth things out at school. He did us both a big favor. For you, it's altar boy lessons. You know what I'm saying to you?"

"Yeah," Mike said without understanding a fucking thing.

He'd remain in one piece for a while. And besides he had the house to himself for the first time in history. He could look through everybody's closets and drawers if he wanted. Or he could oil his glove and throw a ball against the side of the garage and nab grounders. Or watch TV. What was Willie doing today he wondered?

He turned on the TV and waited for it to warm up. Fuzzy black and white images appeared, he adjusted the antenna. There was Bishop Fulton J. Sheen, speaking as he did each week. Mike liked Bishop Sheen, not because he understood him, but because he seemed like a real nice guy and he made people laugh.

Every once in a while he'd ask a question or make a statement, then he'd walk to the camera and look right at you, waiting for what he said to sink in.

Beside him was a blackboard with words and arrows pointing everywhere. The topic was the Infallibility of the Holy Father, and the joy of being Catholic in today's uncertain world. He was caught in a rapture. On a roll.

Mike was thinking. The priest had out-moved him. Again. The ugly prick had the balls to come to his house and put on a brilliant, hour long dog and pony show, bullshitting about altar boys and saving souls. Fuck him. This was serious shit and Mike was getting nervous. Even more nervous than the fight the day before, because this wasn't a fight of the usual kind. He shuddered. If he wasn't very careful he could quite literally become a sex slave on a prison planet.

Mike noticed that Fulton was modeling a simply divine silk gown, long and flowing with a darling matching cap, informing his devoted flock of how often and how badly they'd offended and their odds of 'Getting In'. Mike checked under the gown for high heels.

Sunday passed slowly and unhappily.

Chapter 9

HE HAD HIS mind on other things and didn't catch it right away. The stink was wafting around the room and kids were holding their noses and snickering. The Blade was at her desk checking weekend homework tallies when it hit her.

She stood, marched to the front of the platform, cleared her throat and bellowed, "Who's had an accident? Which one of you? I want to see a hand."

She waited a long few seconds for an answer. It smelled like the whole first row had shit their pants at the same time. Some kids had buried their faces in the crook of an arm and appeared to be on the brink of mutiny.

"Henry, would you open the back door, please?" Henry got up with a suppressed grin on his face and did as asked.

Every once in a while some scared shitless kid did it, too terrified to ask permission to go to the bathroom. It happened. Who knows why, but they just sat in their seats and unloaded.

Poor Tommy Cassidy raised his hand and stood.

Tommy stuttered. Once in third grade he was called upon to recite the alphabet. When he got to F he said it about forty times in five seconds, nearly biting off his lower lip, and the entire class had laughed at him. He turned bright red, cried a river, and Tommy's public speaking career was over before it was even a dream. He never opened his mouth in class, or anywhere else, again. Ever.

Tommy stood as if awaiting a verdict. His head hung to hide his tears. The entire class regarded him now as no more than a silly sideshow. To be laughed at and heckled. Mike felt the tortured soul and watched what was left of Tommy roll up and disappear.

Six aisles away Mike noticed Virginia O'Day roll her eyes skyward endorsing her disapproval, mumbling her disgust and then laughing. And still The Blade kept Tommy on display.

Mike perceived a powerful force. A hatred he could not pinpoint but one he couldn't shake. It might have been sympathy for Tommy, the blinding rage of injustice, his own fear of aiding a fellow human being in despair. Or a mix of all. Or maybe it was not walking boldly across the room to Virginia O'Day and strangling her at her own God damn desk. Whatever it was it stuck to his gut like cheap beef and would not dissolve. Nevertheless, he did not act but only endured the terror Tommy experienced.

"Thomas, for Heaven's sake go home and get yourself cleaned up," the Blade snickered.

No doubt about it. Tommy was full of shit all right. He was up to his hips in it. With his pants packed he walked down the aisle toward the cloakroom as every student watched and those nearby turned their heads away, laughing and grimacing from the awful odor.

Oddly Mike wondered, would he pull Virginia O'Day from quicksand and certain death if the situation ever arose.

The week came and went. Mike got smacked for looking out the window once but that was it. Tommy didn't return until Thursday and Mike's inclination to entertain the students had all but disappeared.

At home his parents made him say grace every night and the jokes started. They began calling him 'Father K' or 'Cardinal K' after the hi-balls kicked in. His hitting and fielding were suffering and his friends were looking at him funny. Ten year old Mike had things on his mind. The questions were piling up without answers.

Chapter 10

SOMETIMES IT WAS as if you were frozen in ice. Alive but stuck there. You didn't feel the chill or suffer from lack of air. You could walk and talk, and eat and sleep, that was about it. You were maybe a pebble or an old bone or a boulder trapped in ice, a mile from the light. You wanted to move, thought you could, knew you should, but something of your own making, something inside refused to cooperate.

History was most likely bullshit but some of it at least was true. Mike usually read about Davy Crockett and Daniel Boone and Ben Franklin and other guys like that when he was supposed to be doing his homework. To Mike history was an adventure filled with tales of men who melted their own ice. Men who traveled vast distances through hostile territories to affect the lives of total strangers, or to change what never would have happened into something that did.

That's why Mike loved the guys in the white hats on TV on Saturday morning. They took a lot of knocks sometimes, but in the end they beat up the bad guys. They had balls and they talked to their horses.

And he was on his way to altar boy lessons. If he didn't solve this one he faced a very likely possibility, being transformed into a smaller version of Fulton. Not only that, he'd be at the priest's beck and call, and he knew what that meant. Getting chased around the sacristy by a Jane Mansfield look-alike.

Sometimes he spotted the priest's black car driving around with other kids in it, or just one kid. He'd always imagined they were the real smart kids in the parish, holy kids, the chosen few who could do no wrong. He was more curious than envious that he was not included.

He imagined they lived in happy homes with happy people, sailed through school with perfect marks, reaping praise from parents and teachers. That they, not he, were destined for bright futures and great achievement. And that was just the way it was. These were the things he assumed were true.

But now he had other ideas as he walked to church. He was worried. No solution had presented itself. It was Saturday morning and he couldn't get out of it. He tried pleading dumb, that he'd never get the Latin, or know where you were supposed to be with what item and when. But as usual nobody listened, plus they just got pissed off at his protests. His friends would see him on the altar and think he'd gone holy on them. None of the kids at the field were altar boys, and they would soon be gathering to choose sides.

Walking along he couldn't see more than a few feet in front of him. He entertained the idea of asking his grandfather to run interference on the altar boy thing. But he figured there'd be questions and something might slip. Then others might find out and so on and so on. He'd be laughed off the field, forever banished. Word might even get back to Willie one day.

No one must know. Under any circumstances. Ever. It would be the worst possibility. He regretted again not bashing in the bald skull with the gold candleholder.

He walked slowly up the steps of the church and through the open front door. He waited alone, in the back beside the holy water font. He touched the water and blessed himself. This time he meant it.

He recalled the freezing cold Sunday he and Joey had walked to church. For some reason it was High Mass, the place was packed and the altar loaded with priests and altar boys. In the balcony the choir sang. Then, as one hymn ended and the voices of the singers faded, the magnificent piercing tone of a woman took over, rising higher and higher in volume until it filled the building with the most beautiful sound Mike had ever heard. The Ave Maria was sung as if The Supreme Being Himself was conducting his favorite Angel. Mike turned, hoping for a glimpse of the woman. She was out of sight, but the face of every person behind him was washed in serenity.

The sacristy door was closed. In the first two rows sat five kids. Three in the first, two in the second. Mike didn't know any of them. He walked down the aisle, genuflected and slid into the fourth pew. It was quiet and the incense from the week's ceremonies lingered.

Funny it is how the smells, echoes, the stained glass, pews, altars and arches radiate something sacred and spiritual. And how on that radiance ride innate messages of love of one's fellows, hope for peace, hope for better and wiser futures for all, more fulfilling futures. Above it all radiates a doubtless certainty that some form of Supreme Being does indeed exist, and that man would be something far less than man without that certainty.

He noticed that the other kids sat quietly in their seats, and there was no clowning around as kids would do. There wasn't a peep. They all seemed like wooden Indians.

He got a strange feeling. His apprehension was palpable. The priest would be making his appearance shortly and they'd see each other again. Mike was stuck in the ice.

The door opened and the priest made his way across the altar, genuflected at the Crucifix, and walked through the swinging door of the communion rail. He was a few feet from the first pew. He acted as if nothing had ever occurred.

For the first minutes Mike had looked only at the floor, terrified of meeting the eyes. But then the priest began to lecture on the history of Christians and the atrocities they'd endured at the hands of the evil Romans. That brought him around slightly. The priest spoke of kings and crooked politicians who'd opposed the real neat things that Jesus was doing. The early form of Sunday mass was a ritual, conceived in catacombs when the Christians were on the run, dodging the Romans. Catechism, he said, was a Latin word meaning to teach by word of mouth. He described the coded communications they devised to keep the Romans in the dark, and that a lot of them were still in use today. This was originally how the word of God was brought into the world. And despite their fears of being discovered, the early Christians met in those catacombs to listen and to learn. They were taught God's laws and God's virtues, and bravely they went forth into the world and began to spread His Word.

It was so much different from school. The priest spoke as if the church were a university lecture hall. He actually felt like somebody was talking to him for the first time in his life. And it wasn't like you were going to be tested on it or anything. The priest explained the different vestments and what they were used for. And all the vessels on the altar and other stuff, too. You really couldn't do anything but pay attention. You got sucked in.

The priest was a smooth talking son of a bitch, that was for sure. He had to admit it. But he'd seen the other side of him and he didn't care if the priest could teach him to fly. Mike would never spend a minute in a gown on that altar near that fucking freak. Period.

After the lectures only five of the six kids walked down the front steps and went home.

There had to be a way. Lesson number one had ended at least with him still inside of his clothes. But the priest was cunning. Like a predator stalking a meal. There was a perceptible smirk, you could see it if you looked. The whole show was a set up. The priest had boxed him in beautifully and he did it with the ease of a chess master.

Mike could feel his heart sink as his desperation grew, his mind on nothing else. It was a nerve wracked little boy who faced a very scary future. A future under the thumb of a very intelligent pervert. The priest knew Mike could say nothing. What was he gonna say? Who was he gonna tell?

On the way home he practiced his Marty McGuire face. Marty was the kid who got demoted. Maybe if he perfected a Marty face he'd fool 'em all. Marty's mouth was always slightly open, his lips pouted and wet, the lower jaw worked its way side to side a lot,

and he had a fixed dull gaze. And Marty looked like he
could pull a fire hydrant out of the sidewalk. You were
afraid to talk to him or have him sit behind you. Once
Mike caught Marty staring at him but Marty didn't look
away. Marty kept on staring. He was sort of chewing
and staring. Like a cow but creepier. Mike got the idea
he could pull a hatchet out of his desk and chop up
some kids with it. He looked that crazy. After a minute
or so of practicing the Marty face he gave up. His eyes
hurt and he knew nobody would buy it.

"Oh, my God, he's back. My Little Monsignor K is
back from the Crusades. Oh, my gawwwd," his mother
yelled.

She had a hi-ball in one hand and a Chesterfield
in the other and it wasn't even noon. Her hair was in
rollers and her face was plastered with white cream.
The house was as clean as a whistle. You'd think he'd
just been elected to the College of Cardinals the way she
went on.

"Well, how'd it go? What'd you do? How many
kids were there? Did you know anybody? Your father's
going crazy. We're having a party. Everybody's coming.
So how'd it go? Say somethin' will ya. Jeez, Mikey."

"It went okay. Six kids."

"Who ja...? how ja...? what ja...? How many? Just
six kids? Holy smoke! That's all? Well, I guess that
makes sense. Every kid in the parish wouldn't be there.
Would they? Did you learn any Latin? Joey and Denis
were just here. They're at the field. I gotta get ready.
Your father had to go to work but he's dying to know
how it went. And tonight we're having a party."

With that, she was off. Tonight was a week away
but she had to get ready. Mike couldn't get out of there

fast enough. He changed, grabbed his glove and shot out the front door.

He immediately took over as catcher. Joey, Denis, Kenny and Albert were on the field. That was it, not enough for a real game. They were playing 'fuckit'. Whenever their weren't enough kids for fair sides everybody played both ways. You might be in center field but all of a sudden it was your turn at the plate. So you had to run in from center and hit.

Sometimes, when things got desperate, the game was played with 'the imaginary man'. It kept you on your toes. You had to 'remember' there was a man on base when there really wasn't. So kids would yell out "imaginary man on" every so often. And sometimes there were arguments over whether the imaginary man was safe or out or if he scored. You gotta be ten to use the imaginary man.

Joey was at the plate. "Where were ya? You get punished?"

Mike had to admit where he was or make up some shit like he was with his grandfather helping the old guys pull up maple tree roots. Or he got his ass kicked by his old man. Or this or that. The pitch came in high.

"Where'd we get this?" The ball was brand new.

"You won't fuckin' believe it," said Joey.

"What?"

"Denis fouled the old one into the tree and it stuck. Look."

He pointed and there was the old ball stuck up in the tree which served as third base. The old one was black, wound with electrical tape. If it wasn't fouled into the woods and lost, it'd last all summer as long as there was tape. Now it was wedged between two branches way up in the tree.

"So where'd we get this one?" asked Mike.

"Frankie got it for his birthday," Frankie Spinelli was one of the eight year olds.

"Any more kids coming?"

"I don't know. Maybe. Me and Denis went to get you, your mother said you were at church. You taking altar boy lessons or something?"

Shit! Not even time to make up a good lie. Joey seemed a little pissed off or sarcastic. The pitch came in, Joey swung and missed. Then Mike realized his mother must've spilled the beans.

"I had to. My fucking father made me."

"Why?"

"I don't know why. I think he thinks I'm maybe going to hell or something."

Joey swung and missed again. Talking about it made him feel funny because he thought that maybe Joey thought he was smart in school, and nothing was further from the truth. In fact Mike would've died if any of his friends knew how bad his report cards really were. That was bad enough in itself, but the whole topic was too close to the sacristy shit.

The victory over the ugly brothers was becoming a distant memory. Nearly gone now was the awareness of being fully alive, fearless and full of adventure. The victory in the woods had made him acutely aware of many perceptions he knew not he possessed; his emotional state, his muscular tension, balance, heartbeat, Albert's fear, affinity for his friends, the importance of the fight, and more. The clarity of that moment was the highlight of his life. A major win to cherish.

But now his joy of living was being squashed. Suddenly the stinky priest, his bushy eyebrows and weird lips was an image in his head he couldn't shake. Though surrounded by his best friends he couldn't have felt lonelier.

His life hung in the balance and his dim witted parents couldn't be more in the dark, couldn't be more delighted he was hooked up with the priest. If he told them the truth they'd turn on him, not the pervert. But that secret would never see the light of day. They probably figured that his grades might improve or his soul was safe and sound, or he wouldn't be pulling armored car stick-ups when he grew up, or some shit.

The priest was backing him into a corner and Mike found himself up against a nearly faceless enemy. Faceless, in that the priest had so easily bamboozled his parents. Faceless, because of the treacherous guise with which he was able to carry out his most wicked intentions. Faceless because he was a hypocrite and a traitor and no one had the sense or the courage to look beyond the mask.

And faceless, in that shadow boxing was the name of the game. No one had figured out how to get inside and swing at that. And the priest knew it. His very stock in trade was his own brand of mysterious fear he preached weekly. The façade was brilliant. He had half the town convinced that in the blink of an eye they could become murderous or immoral, and that he was the last guardian of that forbidden gate. He was a priest and to his flock he walked on water. His shell was shiny but beneath it lurked a decayed being with wicked perversions and evil intentions.

Mike was stuck in the ice. Joey swung and foul tipped one off Mike's head.

"Shit. You okay?" he heard Joey say.

"Yeah." He shook it off. It actually made him feel better. Not himself but better.

Then Joey looked at him funny. "What's going on?"

"Nothing. Why?" said Mike. Joey only shrugged.

After the game he walked to his grandfather's house. He pined for the good old days where his only problems were dodging The Blade and his crazy old man. He went to the garden but no Pop. The little green house was empty too. He went into the house and from the kitchen he saw him asleep in his old chair with the newspaper on his chest. He watched his grandfather's shallow breathing and he longed to be as carefree. He was tempted to wake him but decided not to. He felt the knot on his head for comfort. He had to go. It was getting close to supper. There was a party tonight at his house.

Chapter 11

EVERYBODY WAS HAMMERED. The first barbe-cue of the season was in full swing. It had come indoors and the place was packed with people gabbing and laughing. Mike's Aunt Harriet and her new boyfriend were jitter-bugging on the living room floor to a guy called Elvis.

He spotted his mother and his mother's friend, smiling at him from across the room. No doubt the word of his altar boy lessons was the topic between those two.

Somebody stumbled and almost knocked over the TV. One of his uncles was trying to talk to a woman but he was so drunk he couldn't.

Another couple was in the corner talking. The guy was looking at her boobs for a few seconds and then whispered something in her ear and they both laughed.

His mother beckoned to him. He figured she wanted him to deliver an update to her and her friend about his new altar boy career. But she just handed him her empty glass and nodded in the direction of the makeshift bar. Then she said, "Mikey, get me a butt too, wouldja."

On the way to the bar the ladies told him how handsome he was and how big he was getting. His Uncle Pete, an engineer with a drink in each hand, slurred a barely audible question in his direction about his plans for college. Mike gave him an 'are you shitting me' shrug and kept walking. He picked a cigarette from a pack on a table.

The bartender was two people, a couple actually, from up the street. He couldn't remember their names. He had to wait in line and was just looking around at the guests. His little sisters were sitting on laps and drinking cokes.

"May I get you something, sir?" said the man.

The couple smiled down at him. Mr. Douglas, that was his name. Mr. Douglas put on a surprised face and said to his wife, "Hey, I know this guy, he's in here all the time." Then he winked at her. "It's Mike, he lives here. Get it? He lives here." Then he said, "Hey buddy, good to see ya. You're outa school soon, right? You must be heartbroken."

"Yeah," Mike laughed. "Hi, Mr. Douglas, hi Mrs. Douglas."

Mrs. Douglas smiled and said, "Hello there, Mike. I see you kids are playing ball at the field already. Bet that makes you happy."

"Yeah," Mike smiled.

"So, what'll it be pal?" said Mr. Douglas.

"Ahm, one high-ball please, light on the water."

Then Mr. Douglas whined from the side of his mouth, "Left hook, light, for the hostess with the mostest. Coming right up, pal."

He went into a comic routine of mixing the drink and then handed it down to Mike. "There you are my good man, enjoy."

"Thanks, Mr. Douglas," said Mike.

He was on his way to his mother when somebody jumped in front of him with a camera. He had a high-ball in one hand and a cigarette in the other.

"Say shit!" She pushed the button. "Ha, gotcha. Take one of us, Mikey, wouldja?" It was his Aunt Harriet.

"Okay, wait a sec." He delivered his mother's goods and then returned to Harriet who was preening herself in her little mirror.

She handed him the camera. "Okay, look through the hole 'til you see us, then press that. On three, okay?"

"Okay." He found the two heads in the little hole.

"Okay, ready? One..." On three he pushed a button and the light flashed. The boyfriend said thanks and handed him a quarter for his troubles. A quarter, beautiful.

Then Mike asked the guy, "Can I get you something from the bar?"

"Great idea, kid. Scotch, straight. And a red wine for the lovely lady."

Mike was back in a flash and the guy handed him a buck. He took an order from his uncle Pete and picked up a deuce.

He hit four in a row like that. He was up ten bucks and the night was young.

Mr. Douglas said he could get arrested for serving minors but was only too happy to put on a comedy skit while filling orders. Mike caught on quick, laughing when he was supposed to and smiling at Mrs. Douglas. But he laughed mostly at how many suckers you could squeeze into one room. He was making about a buck a minute.

He saw Harriet place the little camera on a side table and he also noticed her drink was nearly gone. He brought her a refill and was rewarded.

The drunker they got the bigger the tip. In an hour he was up thirty bucks. Two fives and twenty singles. At this rate he could take the rest of the year off. He kept noticing Harriet's camera on the table.

It was Sunday morning, the morning after. What a crazy party. The joint looked like it was hit by Huns. But Mike had eighty-five bucks from hustling sauce the night before. Unbelievable. He kept counting, hoping for a mistake in his favor but the final tally was eighty five.

He'd have to hide the money and get out of the house soon. His father would be up shortly, hung over and pissed off.

Normally if you were sitting around watching the tube or something you'd get ordered to do something, and if you were doing something you'd get told to sit down and shut up. But the morning after a dozen 'left hooks' the volume and the confusion increased. His mother would find her way down eventually, in a hi-ball haze, and start ranting. That would piss off the old man. The fallout would be brutal but actually it was all quite predictable. He'd come down and smack you around just because you were around, and smack-aroundable. But if you weren't around, well, you weren't around.

As he headed up the stairs to change he again noticed Harriet's camera from the previous night. She'd forgotten it. Mike looked at it for a long moment. Then he went up, changed and got the fuck out of the house.

Mike never got involved in conversations about school, for obvious reasons. But in those days there were a hundred kids an acre and you might run into anything. A kid who'd talk your ear off about geography or arithmetic or some shit. A smart kid, so smart he couldn't find anyone to talk to. So he'd talk to anybody who'd listen. Rare but it happened. Such a kid was Raymond Cromwell.

Mike was walking by as Ray came out of his front door. He was Protestant and went to a different church. Protestant kids seemed different.

Maybe they didn't know they were going to hell. Maybe they weren't saddled with Predestination. Maybe that was a good thing. Maybe that's why his house was so fucking crazy, you worried about it all the time, like report cards. Maybe you found out through the mail when you got old. Maybe you got shit-faced every night and smacked your kids around because the big day was fast approaching. Maybe.

Once in a while Ray showed up at the field to play but he was one of those kids who sort of tagged along when it came to sports. He was husky, wore glasses, had a crew cut and loved to talk about what made things go. One time at the field, when they were in the woods waiting out the rain, he put everybody to sleep by explaining how his gyroscope worked.

This morning he carried his prayer book and a Popular Mechanics mag. The instant he saw Mike he started talking. As they walked along Mike listened to Ray's ideas about solid rocket fuel, stuff the Russians were doing with and without monkeys in space and his own ideas about a manned mission to the moon. He hoped Ray wouldn't want his opinion or ask any challenging questions.

Gravitational forces, atmospheric resistance and a guy named Von Braun kept popping up. He even drew his own mechanical thrust theory with a stick in the dirt. He used words like calculate and velocity and vector as if both were professors theorizing the vast unknowns of space and planning that mission to the moon.

He pictured Ray in a long white coat with a clip board. He was like a mini Mr. Wizard, the science guy on TV. He was so enthusiastic about space travel and gadgets. And Mike just nodded along which made Ray talk even more. He was actually getting the sensation of rocketing through space.

He liked Ray's enthusiasm and his command of the sciences. All in all it was a pretty good walk. Ray invited Mike over to check out his homemade rockets anytime. Mike wondered if they were big enough to fly around in. The image of him dropping water balloons on kids from way above the trees made him chuckle. Or a bucket of tar on Virginia O'Day as she marched arrogantly up the steps to school. He could see himself in an open cockpit, wearing goggles, a scarf and a leather helmet, flying all over the place.

Mike thanked Ray for the invite and they went their separate ways. He wondered about Ray and all the other Protestants going to hell when they died. Ray seemed like such a nice kid. It didn't seem fair.

When to kneel, when to stand, when to sit? Get real. Follow the crowd.

The little girl in front of Mike stood the entire time looking around at people and things. She picked her nose and ate it while looking up at a fat old lady in a flowered hat who was fanning herself. She talked out loud and some people laughed.

She was as cute as a button and new to walking and talking and wanted to show it off. When she got carried away, got too loud, her father's hand gently patted her head and she'd stop for a while.

Mike noticed she didn't flinch or react in fear to his touch. A minute later she started up again and whispered to Mike. "We have ithe cweam."

Mike widened his eyes in mock envy. She acknowledged this with a tight-lipped nod and said "thtwabewwy."

She then bunched up the front of her dress and chewed that, exposing her pink underwear to rows of worshipers. Mike suppressed a laugh, that all this was taking place in church.

Then she mouthed another whisper "nana bwot it." Mike's stomach growled out loud. He made a funny face and the little girl laughed. Her father bent and whispered into her hair and she turned away.

Ice cream! A capital idea. He'd go down the Square and surprise himself. All alone. He had the money. That's when the shit hit the fan.

Chapter 12

MR. K WAS sat at the kitchen table reading the paper, looking like he'd gone ten with Marciano the night before. He lit a butt.

"Where's that kid of yours?" he said sarcastically to his wife.

She mumbled a barely coherent hung-over "In church, where he belongs."

They sat like hung-over eggheads.

"Holy shit", said Mr. K, reading from the paper. "Some nun killed herself the other day. They found her hanging from a fire escape in an alley in Dorchester. Holy shit, same nuns that teach Einstein."

"Teach him what," she whined caustically.

"She was twenty-six and there might have been some hanky-panky going on after hours. A nun. Imagine that? Can you believe it?"

"Let me see that," said Mrs. K in very high interest.

He knew God damn well he shouldn't be eating ice cream in the morning. He hadn't even eaten breakfast. But he had a pocket full of hard earned dollars for the first time in his life. His justification was it would soon be noon and you could eat anything after noon-time.

A mild mental argument ensued. "Are you nuts? You can't be doing this. Why don't you get bacon and eggs? Something that'll stick to your ribs."

"Cuz I want ice cream, that's why."

"But it's not even noon yet."

"So what. I'm doing it anyway. Shut up, will ya."

"Okay. Okay. But don't say I didn't warn ya."

The ice cream parlor was a beauty. Right out of your dreams. It had little round gray marble table tops set in chrome with matching cushioned chairs, a black and white tiled floor with booths off to the side, huge windows and a juke box. Beside the counter was the ice cream display. A dozen colorful flavors in big round ten gallon containers stared back invitingly through the glass partition. On the working wall were shiny metal gizmos for making frappes and milk shakes, anything you wanted.

The aroma of ice cream and hot fudge, thick as fog, did exactly what it was supposed to do to Mike's nose, tongue and intestines. It hoodwinked him, blinded him to all consequences, convinced him that a banana split inside an empty stomach at ten in the morning was completely logical.

The voice in his head spoke at just the right moment. It was the same soft voice that narrated the wild animal segment on the Wonderful World of Disney.

Incredible. Mike loved that show. It laughed reassur-
ingly to him.

"Why, it's the American way, Mike. Don't give it a
second thought. Everyone does it. It's ice cream. It's
okaaaaay. Just order up and take a seat, my boy. Or, if
you prefer, stay right where you are and see for yourself
how it's done by one of our trained professionals."

Absolutely, Mike thought, actually nodding right
along with the voice. It was all so wrong, that it was all
right.

The guy behind the counter, dressed from head to
toe in starched white cotton, checked his watch and
gave Mike a funny look. Stark contrast to the soft
inviting sales pitch in his head seconds before.

Mike ordered.

"Ya sure about this, kiddo? It's not even lunch
time yet."

Mike nodded and the guy got moving. He watched
him slice the banana, lay it in the oblong stainless steel
dish, then scoop out a ball of chocolate and a ball of
thtwabewwy. Over that he ladled hot fudge. It fell thick
and smooth. On top of that four by seven inch felony
was a layer of melted marshmallow, and finally some
crushed walnuts. Mike was practically comatose and
hadn't even tasted it yet.

"Have a seat kid, I'll bring it over to you."

Mike licked his lips and took a seat. A few seconds later the guy arrived and set it down. The metal
dish met the marble table with a click. The very fact
that this nearly was a felony made it all that much
sweeter.

Mike had to stretch, nearly stand up to get to it. If
he was hanging by his feet from a tree it wouldn't have

mattered. He watched the marshmallow and fudge drip off the sides. He started with the drippings first.

His immediate emotion when it hit his tongue was a weird mix of sympathy and affinity for his buddies and his grandfather. Go figure. But the sensation was indescribable physical pleasure. Toss in some reward, ownership, selfishness, don't talk to me now, freedom, sin, a little salvation, and you get the idea.

It took him eleven minutes to make it all disappear. He checked the outside of the dish, where it curved down into the stem, for drippings he may have missed.

Afterwards he sat silently, like the snake that ate the frog. Stuffed. Problem solved. He watched the pedestrians move by the big window. Could they not comprehend what they were missing?

All on its own his mind recalled the banana/hot fudge mix and it lingered awhile. Then the crushed walnut/marshmallow combo took over and that lingered awhile. Then the fresh drippings came into focus. He thought about the roll of cash he sat on.

He compared where he was now to school, and what he had to return to later. He decided he was as happy as could be right where he sat. What a great hideout. And what the hell, it was only another forty-five cents.

"Can I have another one, please?"

The guy's face was in his hands, supported by his elbows as he read the paper behind the counter. He heard the request and looked at Mike.

"You sure about this kiddo?" the guy looked at his watch. "I mean, it's not even..."

"Yeah. One more," said Mike.

The uphill walk was tough, each step a struggle. He may as well have been wearing a space suit. He was feeling kind of dizzy, unhappy, watery inside, and tired.

His stomach began doing flips as he approached the field. He thought about making a run for it to his bathroom, but he could hardly walk.

He made his way to the battleground hoping his spirits would lift, wishing away his agony. He thought of the fight, Joey in the tree and all the fun afterwards. But stomachs have a mind of their own, and Mike's was in no mood for humor of any kind. It was all business, churning two banana splits into God knew what, and searching for a hole to send it through. It wanted revenge.

Ten trees away was Creature, in his usual get-up of tee-shirt, dungarees, engineer boots, garrison belt and piled high greasy black hair. He wasn't alone, he was with a girl, and she was letting Creature have his way with her. His face was bandaged from the fight.

He'd told her a tall tale of being jumped by four other kids after school, that he and Gary had kicked some serious ass, and three of the four were still in the hospital and might never walk again. To further impress the girl he'd brought along a pint of whiskey, now nearly gone, and his usual pack of Pall Malls.

He'd thought of everything but cleaning his finger nails, and breath mints.

Neither was aware of the other's presence. Mike did the human thing and blamed his terrible condition on everybody but himself. He cursed the wad of cash, cursed the antics of Mr. Douglas behind the bar, Harriet and her boyfriend, the drinkers and tippers, everybody he could think of. He was as sick as a dog and about to explode.

He found the right tree and pulled his pants down. Then he got an odd sensation in his jaw, his mouth began to water, the cold sweats hit, and his strength vaporized. He rolled to his right onto all fours with his ass held high and his head hung low. The puke poured out in Technicolor. He vowed he'd never eat ice cream again. Not that much at the same time, anyway. If he lived through this he'd go home to his room and study all day long. He was helpless and sorry for his sins.

Creature heard the noise. Even in the throws of passion it got his attention. It might be a nosey kid or two. He walked a few feet and heard the moans and the puking. Then he saw it. A kid beside a tree on his hands and knees with his pants down to his ankles puking his guts out.

The kid rose to his knees and took deep breaths, bent over and puked again. Creature couldn't see who it was but he thought it was very funny. Some poor kid losing his lunch with his bare ass in the air. What a riot.

The girl made her way over. He put his index finger to his lips, the quiet sign. They watched the stupid kid and laughed silently. The kid's pants were down to his ankles for some reason. Then the kid puked some more.

Suddenly Creature's grin vanished. He passed the whiskey to the girl and took off in a run.

Mike heard stomping and knew it was trouble. He saw Creature and screamed in fright. He tried running and pulling up his britches at the same time. Creature was nearly upon him.

From the corner of an eye he saw the girl.

"You little asshole, I'm gonna kick the shit out of you."

Mike ran in baby steps, trying desperately to hitch up his drawers. Creature sent a viscous but awkward kick to Mike's head. Most of it missed but he saw stars, and his pants were still around his ankles. He willed himself to remain conscious.

Creature wasn't well balanced physically either. The kick had buckled his other knee and he went down. Add high alcohol content, low IQ and it wasn't pretty. The girl laughed aloud, further enraging Creature.

Mike took advantage of the precious seconds to get his pants up properly but his underwear wouldn't cooperate. They were rolled into rope below his knees so he couldn't get his pants above them.

The girl's howling laughter was now a steady backdrop to the pathetic picture. But embarrassment was the least of Mike's problems now.

Creature was off the ground with a big stick in his hand. He banged a tree several times to make his point.

Mike pegged a rock but it missed. He put the tree between himself and Creature. An obstacle he hoped to buy time with. Mike had his hands full, trying not to puke, unwinding his knotted underpants and holding Creature at bay.

Round and round the tree they parried. Mike thought of making a mad dash for safety but deleted it quickly. He'd be caught from behind and pummeled.

The girl was bent over laughing. After all Mike was nearly naked, with his pants practically welded to his shoes and dancing around a tree for his very life. A cinematographer's dream.

"Can you believe this, Wendy? Ha, ha, we see your dick," he laughed. Then Creature turned mean.

His stinky booze breath hung in the air. "I'm gonna cut your balls off and run this stick up your ass. A whole bunch of times, wise guy. I owe you for this," pointing to his face.

"You liar," said Wendy. "You said five hockey players jumped you and your brother down the Square."

Creature took a giant step sideways, hoping for an advantage, but he slipped and fell. Instead of rising quickly he got a funny look on his face. He sniffed, then lifted his hands slowly.

From his finger tips to his elbows ran a thick oozing combo of dead leaves, stomach acid and two half-digested banana splits.

"Oh, jeezuz. What the fuck!" He looked at the back of his pants. "Holy shit, it's puke. I'm covered. Jeezuz!"

Mike unwound his underwear, got his pants back on and hightailed it out of the woods.

"Wendy, help. Wendy." But Wendy had stopped laughing and was backing away, on the verge of gagging, at the sight of Creature. "Come on, where you going?"

"You're a liar. And you're disgusting. Don't ever call me again, Creature. I can't believe this."

"Don't call me that."

He hid in the cellar. Lucky and humiliated, that's how he felt. Lucky that Creature couldn't hit a Buick two out of three times with his running kicks. And humiliated that the girl had witnessed his up-down Abbott and Costello skit of covering his dick with his tee-shirt, unraveling the knot his underpants, and avoiding Creature at the same time.

The more he moved the harder Wendy laughed. If his friends had caught that act he'd have been on the next train for the coast. It was terrible. It would be a while before he convinced himself none of that really happened at all.

He thought of Tommy Cassidy's 'accident' in school and, for the moment, felt like a blood brother. He was still a little sick and had a welt on his head from Creature's boot.

But he felt hungry, which was probably good news.

He sat at the kitchen table with a bowl of cereal and searched the sports section for the latest on #24. The house was empty, most likely all at church. He wandered from room to room and worried. He had the 'what ifs' real bad. Creature would be in a rage all summer. That nut might do anything.

His father could arrive at any second and start smacking him around. The Blade was always a threat. He had homework due the next day that somehow had to be ignored. The priest wasn't going away, and the altar boy thing, with his proud parents unwittingly in league with the priest, were big worries. It was all too much.

Harriet's camera, he noticed again, was right where she'd left it. He tried to recall the instructions she'd given. What's this thing? What's that thing? Do I spin it or push it? Who would know?

It appeared in the blink of an eye with consequences too terrible to contemplate, like the fight in the woods only ten times worse. If he could get it to work, if he had the courage to use it, he might be able to save his skin.

His enemy would do no less. His enemy, after all, wasn't the dumb and awkward Creature. It wasn't even the Blade or his old man. All they could do was smack you around and screw up your weekend. That was just shit you had to put up with in life. The reward for surviving them was playing baseball with your buddies.

The real enemy was a dangerous and cunning assassin in the guise of a priest. That one could take your soul. That one could screw up your eternity.

Chapter 13

STEVEN QUINN DEVLIN was a very tough Irish immigrant turned coal miner from Pittsburgh. Very tough indeed was this man Devlin. He lived in the days when law and order was determined by fast fists and powerful shoulders. When the Labor Unions were serious ideas in the minds of men and the talking stages had graduated into murderous brawls. These were the early days in the movement, when a notion was given life one day that real live men were not someone's property. The seed took root, the conflict was born, and the Barons of Industry found themselves locking horns with very desperate men.

Devlin was neither an idea man nor a smooth negotiator. He hated the Barons and what they stood for. His craft was terror, this usually accomplished by his mere presence. He delighted at the prospect of beating the hired opposition, or anyone for that matter, into pulp. It didn't matter which side. Fear was his stock in trade. His wisdom in the ways of the world began and ended with broken teeth, jaws, bones and skulls. He was happy in his work. So happy in fact that he took it home with him.

His wife was Mary Devlin. Mary McQuade, before her marriage to Devlin, was a beautiful blonde and green eyed lass with a ready smile for all. She'd come to America with her cousin Madeline who had distant relatives in Pennsylvania with whom they would live.

Maddy, however, had met a boy on the boat and it was love at first sight. The boy was bound for his own distant relatives in Boston to work and to study engineering. So it was with deep regret that Maddy had abandoned Mary at the very hour of their landing in America and gone off happily with the man of her dreams. So much for their plans of a life long friendship.

Within a year, at the tender age of seventeen, she'd fallen for the tall dark Devlin and soon they were married. Shortly a son was born and Mary was as happy as an Irish girl could be. But it wasn't long before her husband's dark side emerged and her perpetual grin had disappeared. It was a fast and deep slide.

Poor Mary had one foot in the nut house from the rages and the beatings meted out over the years to herself and her two sons. Her first born had met a tragic end as an eight year old from a mysterious fall down the flight of steps in their cold, dark house. And it was a broken hearted woman whose only duty in life now was to protect her remaining child, young Steven.

Pale and frail was young Steven from the day of his birth. 'Twas as if he knew what he was being born into and wanted no part of it. He wouldn't come out.' Mary had remarked to a friend.

Years of abuse from other quarters didn't help matters. The nuns and the priests had 'done their best' to toughen him up, but to no avail. Dubbed 'Pinky' by his school mates he became the brunt of their jokes, and at times their punching bag. But he took all they could dish out, like a martyr, remaining stoic throughout.

A pack of rowdies had transformed him into a soccer ball one afternoon, breaking four of his ribs, an arm, causing a severe concussion, leaving him half dead on a chilly wet field until the wee hours of the next morning.

One of the students had told her father just before bedtime of the incident and he in turn had walked two miles to report it to the police, so young Steven was found in the nick of time. Snatched at the very threshold of death's door, he was.

A month in hospital returned him to health but not happiness. His father had stopped visiting the boy after his own investigation had revealed he'd not fought back or even attempted to defend himself. This revelation coming from one of the perpetrators himself.

Upon the boy's return home the father forbade him to attend school or leave the house for fear his fellow miners might discover to whom he belonged.

And so it was for some years that Mary and young Steven cooped themselves in a stark, threatening and gloomy little home, adrift on the stormy sea of perpetual fear. Two lost souls clinging to a lonely and frightening existence.

Mary, by this time, had evolved into a dangerous mix of personalities. Each with color, shape, sound, location, thought patterns, artistic skills, etc. etc. They vied for dominance, shouted orders, sought forgiveness, granted forgiveness, hurled insults, predicted futures, screamed tirades, served as lookouts, told erotic tales and much, much more.

And getting chubby on this psychotic stew was young Steven, not far behind his mother in the 'who's crazier' contest. What a couple of nuts.

The elder Devlin was gaining popularity from the Brains for his talents and persistence in punching the shit out of the bad guys.

Joked one miner on a Friday night to the bar keep, "Oh, they're sure to see things our way. Devlin fills more hospital beds than you pour pints."

The bar keep replied, "But he's not sure which side he's on. In a good many of those beds are our own. And Jazuz, have you heard about that family of his?"

Devlin was making a name for himself, all right. Feared and distrusted he was by all, and hated. He spoke of nothing other than creating more violent chapters in an already turbulent drama. His comments and his jokes were followed with uneasy laughter. He'd hardly mourned his dead son, and all had seen the sorry state of Mary and the boy. But for fear of Devlin they could only watch the decline.

Some had more to gain than others during those times. The union, if successfully formed, would be a bonanza for the Brains but peril for the miners if it failed. The Barons had for years paid handsomely for their interests to be kept intact and for protection. Paid to the very people who were now looking at things through a different pair of rose colored glasses.

The Brains were crime bosses, cops, lawyers, land owners, politicians, press, even some labor leaders, anyone who saw potential profit in playing both sides against the middle. There was much to gain no matter who won. But there had to be conflict. That would ensure a future. They were, in some respect, double agents weighing the strength and determination of both sides, lying in wait to choose the one with the biggest guns.

Those who stood to lose the most were the Barons of Industry and they knew it. Their idea of loss was anything which cut into profits and control. If it was allowed to happen once it would never stop. The writing was on the wall; more demands, less production, higher wages, lower profits, strikes, bribes, new laws, more lawyers, larger payoffs, the whole shebang from a dozen directions. It was time to get down and dirty.

They were wealthy beyond belief. And intelligent. They knew well it was a matter of time before the hungry wolf packs became organized enough to attack. The storm was gathering. How viscous the attacks would be and how much they could withstand remained to be seen. But they were nothing if not viscous themselves. They would share their wealth with no man.

They bought detectives and spies, organized re-placement workers in the event of strikes, and pur-chased small armies to protect their interests and to wage war. If the paupers in the mines worked their lives away for pennies then so be it. To hell with them. And their sons were welcome to do the same. So they planned and schemed, dug in and hunkered down for the fight to come. Fuck the Irish, fuck the Germans and the Poles and the Italians. Fuck all of them. They were hardly American anyway. The Barons would never surrender control.

The country was expanding enormously and with that expansion came an unquenchable thirst for energy. Coal to fire furnaces for steel. Steel to lay track, erect bridges, build cities, to industrialize and to create America. The Barons saw it coming and simply supplied the demand.

In the process they became bigger than the gov-ernment. They made their own laws, held their own courts and had their own penalties. These were the men who built and laid claim to the country and refused to relinquish a single square foot of Her.

Oblivious to these historical dramas shaping America was Crazy Mary, as she was now known. She'd been convinced by several of her 'mental advisors' to give sex lessons to her son. Way ahead of her time was Mary. Her husband's services, whatever they happened to be, were taking him over hill and dale, so he was gone far more often. Days at a time.

She wasn't complaining, and neither was Steven Jr. In fact it was a bonus in many ways. Less of him, more dollars and so more food which suited everyone. And much, much more time.

An idle mind, it's been said, is the devil's work-shop. And no statement was truer than in Mary's case. She'd often teach Steven sewing and crocheting while completely naked, or mockingly scold him as he knitted and purled, and then burst into apologetic laughter calling him a silly boy. She'd dance and sing or cook or bake. She'd swing her long blonde hair and coo in his ear. She'd giggle, as if with girlfriends, about penises and asses, casually describing the pleasures of sex as if it was a recipe for apple pie.

And Steven was an apt pupil. Thin and frail, he made an excellent model for the shawls and dresses she sewed and an excellent companion in bed. Thus they filled the void of time, replacing the grim reality of a lonely existence, a brutal husband and father, with a cozy, colorful universe fashioned by the voices in their heads. Crazy as bed bugs, the two of them.

The immigrants, meanwhile, toiled in desperation and prayed for a break. Contrary to rumors in the old country, the streets of America were not paved with gold. Unsafe conditions in the mines and mills and factories bred illness, accidents, depression, early death, child labor, and grim futures. This was life. There was no plan B for the immigrant. Immoral though it was, the foundation of industrial America was laid.

Morals are codes of good conduct laid down out of the experience of the race to serve as a uniform yardstick for the conduct of individuals and groups. Working a man half to death for another man's great profit, for instance, seems immoral. But in the long run it might be proven otherwise if it was seen to have secured, for a culture, prosperity and many future generations. And if those great profits helped ensure a culture's future there would be little cause for argument.

But if it becomes clear the profiteers have harmed the society it would then be unreasonable not to protest. However, settling difficulties with sane solutions thus avoiding much misery is not something man shines at. In the heat of the moment violence rules and little else makes sense. So battles rage and history is written with its conflicts and its characters.

Within all great movements, however, lesser dramas unfold which have more to do with justice than with morals.

One night an over-zealous employee of the Barons fired shots into a throng of men, killing one of them. The dead man had a wife and four children. He was on his way home and stopped only to join a group who were listening to another man speak his mind on the problems of the day, as men do. It was a needless and foolish assault. Even the Barons showed a softer side and the two adversaries met. The dead man's family must be compensated. The Barons balked. A head must roll. Forget about that they said. It was a mistake, an accidental discharge. They would not sacrifice one of their own. They'd tie it up in court for years and no one would see squat.

But the Brains sweetened the pot with a nice surprise. They too had an overzealous soldier that just had to go, and they would set him up to take the fall for the killing. A beautiful thing said the Barons and agreed to fill the hat for the fatherless family. Who is this guy and what's he done, they asked. None of your beeswax was the reply. Just get us the gun that killed our man and read the papers. So the meeting ended happily with both sides wishing the other a pleasant day.

The gun was procured and hidden in the right place, whereabouts of certain people the night of the murder were rearranged, witnesses and a motive were created. Devlin himself nearly believed the charge of murder against him, so expertly was he set up. The trial lasted a week, he was found guilty and hanged a month later. Problem solved.

But poor Mary and her son were a different kettle of fish. What does one do with such unfortunate people?

It wasn't long before a proposal surfaced. All agreed that Mary was nuts and might benefit by being among other nuts in a place run by more nuts. So off she went one day, all giggles and smiles, never to be seen again.

But the boy's only hope was the infinite mercy of God Himself. After all, sired by a condemned criminal and... well, no one could quite describe Mary anymore. A newspaper account came close, 'an abnormal and forgotten victim driven permanently mad by the death of her child and years of brutality at the hands of her evil husband'.

So it was arranged that the mixed up, shook up kid be put on a train, sent west and placed under the care of dedicated Roman Catholic priests.

As luck would have it, someone knew someone who had a relative in a seminary in Nebraska. The townsfolk, God bless them, had done what they could with what they had and off the boy went as well, never to be heard from again. Over and done with was the Devlin chapter in a small Pennsylvania mining town.

Chapter 14

A MAN EMBARKS on a journey of rational inquiries into religious matters and questions, with the hope of attaining the wisdom he seeks, with a further intention of using such wisdom to help his fellow man attain happiness in this life and the hereafter. An admirable adventure. He joins others on the same journey. They obey the rules, learn discipline, suffer the flesh, all in the hopeful direction of one day acquiring spiritual wealth. Most who journey are decent of character and pure of purpose. But this is no guarantee of success. This is a journey which raises more questions than it answers but that is the journey. And the danger.

Too many questions with too few answers is to sooner or later suffer despair. From there the unfortunate traveler descends into hopelessness which descends further into the pretense of knowing, the pretense of certainty. And below this is the level of pretending one is not pretending. A most dangerous state of mind. Certain it is then that the wrong road on the journey will be taken.

In the shadows of this road lurk the merchants of fear, decadent beings whose mission is to lead astray, crush hope and pervert all decency in the human spirit.

Undetectable, yet very convincing, they hang the signposts directing the unwary down 'salvation road'.

A road mined with spiritual booby traps of blame, shame, regret, dishonesty, addiction, perversion, and above all more secrets. The traveler spends his years thereafter combating the lot and losing every battle.

Near the end of this road is developed a fierce resistance to everything he considers bad or evil. To the great satisfaction of the merchants.

At the end of this road is the blind alley of becoming the very things he resisted, since to resist is to become. Certain now that the wrong road is the right road, he justifies each transgression with a dozen more. The temptations he once sought to conquer have now become his master. The very reason for his journey, forever lost. He rails and accuses, sees sin everywhere, in everyone.

Consumed by these beliefs he cries in the night for losing his battles and his way, since to resist is to become.

Trapped in a web of ignorance and confusion, the traveler is now far worse off than before his journey began. If one was looking for hell and found this turn in the road it would certainly serve. The graveyard of a great many good and decent souls. Since to resist is to become.

So it was that young Steven's arrival with his original sin, his scars and his secrets, was welcomed with wide open arms.

In the woods was the seminary. Miles from any sign of civilization. In the woods with other boys and men who prayed, studied and fasted. Men and boys who punished themselves, and each other, cleansing their souls and washing away their sins.

Over the years he learned to grow fruit and vegetables and to cure meat. He became skilled in carpentry, versed in classic literature, science, theology and mathematics. He studied Greek, Latin and Spanish and spoke them fluently.

He learned self abasement and humiliation. He learned early and well resistance to all temptations of the flesh and the pain of failure. He learned to hide his failures by punishing himself and others. Resisting and failing, and falling further with every attempt until resistance became futile, and life itself merely a clever campaign of hiding his secrets and sins.

His specialty, a skill of which he was most proud, was the art of the well placed fact — the whispering campaign. His particular joy was causing catastrophe and seeing another blamed and punished.

He delighted in witnessing the downfall of anyone, kind or cruel. He'd mastered the black arts of twisting truth, control through fear, and concealing his sins by accusing others of the same sins. The age old ruse of accusation, create guilt. All were guilty and none forgiven without his nod.

More years passed. He grew into a man saddled with secrets and the dark moods of depression. His waking hours bedeviled by the 'terror of being discovered' for his sins of the flesh, such was the burden of his secrets. His soul was a haunted house. When he slept it was with the hope he would not awaken.

Chapter 15

A DREAM IS the imagination gone wild and wacky. It's a frantic effort to orient oneself, to locate oneself, to feel secure, to make sense of real life, find a little truth in a world with very little of it.

Truth by the ton can be found inside any skull. There is, in reality, very little truth to these 'truths'. Call them potential energy dots floating around in there waiting to be energized. They could be tidbits from a book, a movie, a conversation, a lousy situation, anything. Sometimes these dots come loose at night, fuse with one of those conversations or situations, and voila, absolute nonsense.

Nuttier still is the effort by some to interpret these... fusions. However described, they're as wacky as the wind. Flying to school, talking trees, underwater walks, fun falls from skyscrapers, and honest politicians seem normal and everyday. Not unlike the mental process of the average person on the street at noon. But at noon there are distractions, like work, lunch and other people. At night, while asleep, there are none.

Mike was no exception. He was in the woods with his glove on his left hand, a bow in his right with a quiver of arrows slung over his shoulder. He was minding his own business, just looking for some Indian kids to play with.

Sitting around a camp fire was Humphrey Bogart, Willie Mays, Creature, Gene Autry, Harriet and The Blade. They were doing what cowpokes do, drinking coffee, eating beans and listening to Gene sing. But there was no sound to his music and all the faces had blank stares.

The Blade was whittling a piece of wood with a butt dangling from her lips, Bogey sat as quietly as a cardboard cutout. Willie gazed skyward as if expecting a fly ball, and Creature was an altar boy. Gene stirred a huge pot of beans with his rifle and Harriet stared at her reflection. Joey and Denis, with blank faces, pointed up third base at the taped ball. But it wasn't a ball. It was Mr. Cooper, stuck between two big branches.

Gene's horse, Champion appeared, done up in fancy leather and metal studs, and its mane was nearly to the ground. Now the Blade was at her desk in her black habit, where a moment before she was a wood whittling, cigarette smoking cowgirl. Then everybody passed in their homework.

The Blade now wore a bikini, rolls of her flesh were everywhere as she applied lipstick to her whole head with Harriet's mirror. A horrified Bogey pulled out the slingshot to protect himself. He fired point blank, but what flew across space were scoops of 'thtwabewwy' ice cream in the shape of baseballs all of which found the Blade's mouth. Hot fudge and marshmallow dripped from tree trunks forming a pool and Creature waded into it holding a chalice.

Then the priest made his grand entrance. He was riding Champion side-saddle, dressed in a skirt, high heel boots and a pink ten gallon hat. His eyebrows were enormous. Beneath the hat was the long blonde wig and a mouth smeared in red lipstick. He held a pistol.

"Heee, haaa. Have some faith, y'all." He started firing. From the muzzle sprayed not bullets but little boys underpants. They hung in the air like giant snowflakes.

"I'm all right, rodeo fans. Nope, nothing wrong here. Is it making sense yet? Any of it? Oh, what a world we live in. Am I right or wrong? Heee, haaa. Keep the faith, y'all."

Then Harriet walked up with her camera and said, "Say shit." And they all did as instructed.

He awoke under a cloud of worry. It was Monday and, as usual, his homework wasn't done. He had the whole weekend but never touched a book. He silently cursed himself, then began manufacturing lies and excuses, none of which anyone in their right mind would believe.

Marty McGuire once used the excuse that a really strange wind had come along and taken his homework to heaven. He said it with such conviction that the kids wanted more details. But the nun, built like a fucking rhinoceros, didn't buy it and she beat Marty half to death in his seat. She vice gripped his hair with both fists, screaming and yanking, like a woman possessed, until Marty's head had nearly come off in her hands. During the beating he'd changed his story, to the old standby, that his dog had eaten it. She beat him some more and then dragged him out of his seat to the platform beside her desk, where he stood quite visible to all.

She produced a large sketch of smiling skeletons with horns on their heads whipping hell's new arrivals as fire raged around them. That was passed slowly from student to student. For those five minutes she held tight to Marty's hair, howled his damnation, and delivered a brief weather report. The temperature in hell rose in the summer. No bullshit, hell gets even hotter in summer. By the hair of his head she marched him back to his desk and started on the poor little guy again. Then Marty began to puke. He covered his desk, doused a couple of kids, got some on her, was beaten again and forced to clean it all up, while the rage continued.

Mike expected no less, and the clock was ticking. His mouth went dry, his appetite vanished. He'd fucked up and only a miracle would save him from the Blade. What a world.

From downstairs he heard his mother crying. His eyes widened with realization. He'd been expelled, just minutes ago, for incurable stupidity and misbehavior. There was no other possibility. And in the nick of time, too. The Blade had called to inform Mrs. K that someone else had Mike's old seat. Any second now the fallout would start. *"Mary Mother of God, what the hell have I given birth to? Why can't he be like normal kids? He's as thick as a brick. He gets it from your side, you know. You're brothers are all morons. What'll the neighbors say? Oh, God. What will the neighbors say?"*

He'd agree with everything. He'd have to fake tears. *"God, help me. How could it have come to this? How?"* He'd think of something. He could pull that scene off. He could do it.

They'd have a field day at school with his old report cards and test scores. The Blade would hold them high, an example of how not to do it. She'd tape them to the blackboard, turning the joint into a mini museum. The entire school would file by and view them like artifacts from a bygone civilization. *"Look, it's true, he never passed a thing. Look at this one! All zeros! How stupid can a kid get?"* They'd celebrate, get the afternoon off. Virginia O'Day would lead the jeers of his departure with a speech.

His father would be up shortly to beat the shit out of him. He'd spend the day in the cellar thinking about it, until the old man returned from work for round two.

But fuck it. Everything was back to normal. No more altar boy lessons. The priest, a thing of the past. The Blade, a memory. Just baseball, all summer long. Tomorrow he'd show up at Joey's school and surprise him. It was a brand new world; he was coming back to life. He could feel it in his throwing arm. A familiar tune buzzed around his skull, 'Happy days are here again, da-da-da-da..." The thought of going to the same school as all his friends, maybe even the same class as Joey, made him sizzle with exhilaration.

He cracked open his door. He could see his mother sitting on the couch crying, his father standing nearby. What a couple of dopes. They'd never get the big picture, never see what he was out from under.

His mother bent at the waist and let a good cry rip. That wasn't right. It didn't seem to fit the occasion. By now the shame should've turned to rage. They should be pounding their way upstairs screaming like pirates, looking for answers. As if he had any. Instead his father stood and made his way to the stairs. Mike silently closed his door to get ready for the belt. The footfalls were heavy and purposeful. The old 'moments before the execution' feeling hit him. Mike backed into a corner. The door opened to an unsmiling face.

"Your grandfather died early this morning."

His father kept talking but Mike was deaf to it, his head swimming. His mouth opened and his hands dropped to his sides. The smiling Irish face under the thatch of white hair was gone. No more pleasant dinners over stories told in the soft Irish brogue that warmed his heart. No more Friday Night Fights or sharing laughter at the antics of Amos and Andy. Not that he followed them, but Pop never missed an episode and Mike loved to listen to his laughter. They'd eat ice cream after the dishes were dried and put away, then sink into their chairs and watch TV until the network signed off and the test patterns filled the screen.

All that was now a memory. His friend was gone. The only grownup who didn't give him any shit was gone. He began to cry where he stood.

His father gritted his teeth, held up a fist and walked forward.

"Knock that shit off. You hear me? What I tell you about crying?"

Mike shuddered and suppressed his grief.

Mr. K left. Mike only stared out his window. He heard the front door close. Shortly the car started up and sped away. His knees knocked from the threat and the news. No more summer gardens, no more winter deliveries of warm leftovers. No more Saturday morning adventures with Pop's buddies. It was all over and the emptiness hurt like hell.

His sisters were still asleep. He made his way slowly downstairs to see his mother balled up and crying on the couch.

"Hi mum," said a tearful Mike.

"Oh, Mikey, come here." She hugged him and cried deeply. "Pop's gone to heaven. He was taken early this morning. We just found out. Jim Carty found him and came by. Your father and Jim are doing what needs to be done with the funeral home and all. Jim thought he was napping in his old chair and... oh God, Mikey, why now? I just wish..." She let go a good long cry, so did Mike.

Big Jim had found him in his armchair an hour earlier and driven over with the news. They were to go to Cambridge this morning to help somebody with something and pick up a few bucks for their labor. Instead Jim would spend the day delivering bad news and preparing to bury his friend of sixty years.

Now he sat by his friend and whispered through tears to Tom O'Bannion. "We've not long Tom, before..." He suppressed his tears. "So I'll say what I want and leave you in peace. I don't have long meself, so I won't be forgettin' what a friend you been to me and to all of us here, now, and back then. And I know you're sick of hearin' it but I'm saying it anyway. Thanks Tom, for savin' me life from them bloody Brits. I'd made me peace that night. There'd be no tomorrows for Jim Carty. I was a dead man, I knew that. And then..." Jim closed his eyes, blessed himself and cried hard. "You did what you did to them bastards and... got us the hell out. Alive. 'Them Days' made cowards of us. All but you, Tom. It was my pleasure always to be near you. I wish you a pleasant journey and much happiness. I'll watch the boy so no harm comes his way. I promise you that, Tommy."

The screen door from the rear of the house opened and shut with a crash and Mr. K made his way slowly into the living room to greet Jim. Jim stood, a full six inches taller, and they shook hands.

He knew from conversations over the years how Tom O'Bannion regarded his son-in-law, his drinking and his heavy hand with his son. He knew of his displeasure with his daughter Claire. He knew Tom had watched out for the boy in every way he could without refereeing the whole bloody marriage. It had hurt him deeply to know the beatings the boy was taking. He'd told Jim of the welts he'd seen on the boy's back and neck, the fear in his eyes when near his father.

"Well this stinks, doesn't it. He was a kind old man. We all liked him a lot," Mr. K managed.

Jim watched him looking at the body and immediately disliked the man. Here was a man who would never recognize courage, who had faith in everything and everyone but himself. He was a frightened little man and it oozed from his pores.

"He was a man loved by many but feared by none. We did what he asked, because he was a great man. A kind and courageous man. Believe me, you'd want him on your side in a fight, Mister Kilgallen. He saw that in your young Mike and he loved the boy for it."

Jim then leaned down and whispered. "If he thought anything, I mean anything, was being done to harm the boy..."

The statement floated in the room while he watched the eyes and lips.

A vehicle squealed to a stop in front of the house. "Well, that'll be the wagon to take my friend away." Jim nodded in silence. "We been friends since the age of Mike, did you know. Sixty years. Imagine? You would not believe what we seen, Tom and I. Horrific things, Mister Kilgallen. The 'Uprising', many deaths and much grief. Like it or not we found ourselves in the middle and fortunate we were to have him on our side."

There was no mistaking the undertone. Mr. K swallowed nervously.

"There was a man in our little town in Ireland, when we were lads, Mister Kilgallen, who beat his own son with a belt night after night, for years, until the boy one day finally went daft in the head. He was a wonderful little fellow. One cold, dreary night somebody took a knife to the father and filled him with holes, Mister Kilgallen. They never caught the man who did it because they didn't want to. It's how things were done then. Can't say I disagree."

Jimmy donned his skally. "We'll be seeing you at the wake then. Mister Kilgallen." And he walked slowly away.

Mr. K rubbed his chin with a shaky fist. Then he looked at the peaceful Tom O'Bannion and wondered what the fuck kind of life his father-in-law had led.

Chapter 16

'TWAS A GRAND and beautiful Irish send-off on a beautiful June morning. At the grave, after the ceremony, the old Irish women gathered in little groups talking among themselves. The men did the same. They'd come from far and near to say goodbye to Tom. The men that Mike recognized were men he'd met on those Saturday morning adventures with his grandfather.

A short distance away under the shade of a tree was Jim and five others. Jim towered over them as they gazed about and smoked. Mike stood alone observing people and conversations. He noticed that Jim and his group were looking directly at him. Jim then made his way over.

"Mike, some of your grandfather's friends would like to meet you."

The men wearing hats took them off as he and Jim approached. Jim introduced each man. They offered short bows, smiles and strong rough hands with pleasant greetings in thick Irish brogues. Their names were O'Brien, O'Sullivan, O'Donavan, Murphy and McMahon. Mike glowed in the admiration.

"We're all very sorry about this, Mike," said O'Brien.

The others nodded.

"Strong as he was, the Lord saw fit to take him from us," McMahon said

"Mike, no matter the time or the weather, if help was needed he was at our door," O'Donavan said

"Right you are, Pete," said the others respectfully.

"Never one to leave you in need," said O'Sullivan.

Praise and stories of the charity of Tom O'Bannion went on for some time. Mike got the distinct impression that these men had known one another for reasons other than pulling up roots in each other's back yards. There was an unspoken bond among them somehow.

Murphy gazed off in the distance and snickered. "Why, its 'knife in the back' himself. Over there, Jimmy."

"Look at him smiling, would ya. Must be runnin for somethin," said O'Donavan.

"Rat catcher," someone said.

"Not a mark on his soul. Holier than thou. Am I right or wrong boys?" said another.

All laughed.

"You see that man there?"

Jim pointed to a bent and wrinkled specimen among a group of women.

"A treacherous little bugger, that one. Kick a man when he's down. Fill your head with lies about good people. 'Pat Mac, knife in the back' we call him. Your grandfather despised him."

"Turn you over for a quarter, he would," said McMahon.

"And did just that many a time," Murphy said.

"He's a viper, all right," said O'Sullivan.

In the distance a black car rolled slowly toward the gathering. It stopped and the priest got out.

"Here's the real trouble now," said O'Brien.

The faces went cold. Though seventy he was thick and powerful. He stared hard and bared his teeth. The others grunted their disgust as the priest got out of his car. Jim shook his head at the sight of it.

"Watch him now, boys," said Murphy. "He'll go directly to 'knife in the back'. The old ladies will smile as if they're in the presence of the Almighty Himself. Jazuz."

That's exactly how it happened. He then visited Tom's family, bowed his head in mock sorrow, sprinkled some sympathy, and chatted with Mrs. K.

"Ever the politician," said McMahon.

"Boys, I'll be getting young Mike back," said Jim.

They bid their good-byes and Mike did the same.

Jim stopped a short distance from the main gathering.

"There are them you'd do well to watch with a keen eye." He pointed to the priest and Pat Mac. "You're to keep your distance from them, Mikey."

Jim stared as if Devlin were a loose wild animal.

"Carry the soul's plague, they do."

This spoken slowly as if a reminder to himself.

Jim missed Mike's nervous shudder.

Mike was breaking down. The loss of his ally might have been the last straw, but for reasons known only to God and himself he maintained his visions of hope. He'd come close to telling Jim the whole story. Very close. But the secret had to be kept. How on earth could that ever be told?

"Mikey, we're your friends. Your grandfather loved you dearly. If you need me, call or come to the house. It's a short walk. Soon I'll tell you about Tom O'Bannion. What a man he was. Remember, Mike, anything you need. Okay?"

"Okay," Mike said forcing a smile.

"I promised your grandfather."

"Okay."

Jim nodded and then gazed in the direction of the priest. His head shook slightly. He smiled again at Mike and walked back to his friends.

Though well aware of their presence, Mr. K never looked in the direction of Jim Carty and company. As Mike walked back he saw a tightness on his father's face and felt a chill. He looked back at his new friends and waved.

He counted his allies. He would call Jim only if absolutely necessary. But the secret could never be told, so in reality he had no one. He was literally surrounded by an enemy whose most lethal weapon was its own fear and stupidity, a nearly impenetrable barrier. Dumb and lumbering though it was, it was still an army. His own parents part of the rank and file. He had no weapons, no plan, no men. He was it. He was outnumbered, outgunned and outsmarted. He gazed through the mourners to see the smiling priest among his adoring troops of fat gabby women and thin silent men.

He walked a short distance and squatted behind a headstone, out of sight to all. Maybe this was life in the big city. Maybe you were supposed to get pounded into shit so when you grew up you did the same thing. Maybe baseball and fucking around in the woods really were sins. Maybe happiness was a sin. Another bag of mysteries to chew on. More fucking mysteries than Carter had pills.

A bird landed silently on the headstone in front of him. Mike didn't move a muscle. It turned and looked up in a tree to its baby perched on a branch. It fluttered its wings and peeped nervously. The mother remained silent but beckoned her baby to take the plunge. After a moment of indecision it took off. Mike's eyes widened in anticipation. It flapped its little wings frantically and landed, not so gracefully, nearly plumb from the branch. It hopped around, peeping like crazy, either pissed off it had bought the crazy notion of leaping from the limb in the first place, or genuine exuberance, "Holy Toledo, mum, that was wicked beautiful. Get me back up there. C'mon, let's go, c'mon. Peep-peep, peep-peep, peep-peep."

Which reminded him of the day he'd learned to ride his bike. One of his uncles, beer in hand, had given him a big push. The bike wobbled insanely for half a minute, just missing telephone poles, parked cars and kids. It was a miracle of balance. His uncles and his father fell over themselves laughing. One of them mentioned mind over matter and the Ed Sullivan show and they fell over themselves again. But Mike kept his cool and got it right. Soon he was riding smoothly, smiling widely, and ten feet out of his head. It was the most astounding accomplishment of his young life. But that was long ago in happier times.

The birds hopped away, peeping like mad. Mike never blinked and the birds never saw him. The headstone in front of him read 'CAMERON', with a first name, Leo, dates of birth and death. Mr. Cameron had been born in eighteen eighty and had died in nineteen thirty nine.

The guy was old all right. Mike couldn't get his wits around living that long ago, but he felt at least that old, and he slightly envied the guy in the ground.

He peaked around the headstone. The priest was busy delighting his troops with his presence. Mike recalled the Alamo story. The men inside were outnumbered twenty to one, and not a single man would last the night. Now he knew exactly how they felt. The safe haven of his grandfather's home was gone. He was outnumbered by morons. Morons who would not believe what the priest had done if they'd seen it done with their own eyes. They would simply turn their backs and refuse to look at the truth.

Chapter 17

TOM O'BANNION WAS in the ground and Mike got a break the rest of the week in school because there was a death in the family. Everybody felt sorry for you. You could look out windows, not know stuff, and you were off the hook, invisible as it were. Kids for some reason aren't as affected by death as are adults. There's a resilience to them. But for Mike there was more to the loss than in normal circumstances.

By Saturday things were more or less back to normal except his mother was still crying.

"I got it, I got it!" yelled Howdy Doody. Joey was in center wearing a Howdy Doody mask. He made the catch for out number three and trotted in.

On the log, Mike patted his back pocket for the millionth time. Nearly all of the eighty five dollars remained. He looked around the field, then to the tree line. An ambush from Creature and Gary was always a possibility. The slingshot and a pile of rocks sat securely behind the log just in case. Those assholes might have six-guns or tomahawks. Who knew with them.

"How can you breathe in that thing?" asked Mike.

There was no peripheral vision so Joey turned his whole body.

"Are you a Howdy Doody fan, young fella?"

"Yup."

"I breathe through these holes. Wanna go to the Johnson's pool later? It's filled."

"I don't feel like it."

"Sorry about you're grandfather. That stinks."

"Yeah. Thanks. How'd you get it on?"

"It's not that tight."

"How you gonna get it off?" The Howdy Doody head turned to Mike as if insulted.

"I'm actually gonna pull it off myself, Mike. It's not that tight."

"Can I see it?"

"You're looking right at it."

"I wanna try it on, though."

"It's all spit."

"Where'd you get it?"

"Joke shop down the Square. No altar boy lessons today?"

There were in fact altar boy lessons this morning but he wasn't reminded and didn't volunteer. Nevertheless, Mike didn't like the tone of Joey's question yet felt powerless to challenge it. At the moment Frankie the eight year old could have punched him out.

"Knock it over the fucking fence, Frankie," said Joey as Frankie made his way to the plate.

With a grin Frankie turned and spit on the ground. Then he farted.

"I'll knock this up your fuckin' ass, Howdy." Frankie was beginning to fit right in.

"This is baseball. There's no farting and no swearing," said Joey.

"Imaginary man on," yelled Frankie to everybody as he shot the bird to Joey.

"How much?" Mike asked.

"Zip. I stole it."

"No shit? You better tell that in confession you little bastard."

"I already did, so now it's mine."

Except for high heels the priest was naked. He pranced about, cackling like a nervous girl before a date. He'd stop, get a glimpse in a full length mirror, roll his eyes and continue to prance. He grabbed a pair of tweezers, went to the mirror and started plucking.

"Well aren't you the cutest thing," said the priest.

"Thank you. And you are...?" said the reflection.

"It's me, you bitch, Samantha."

"For heaven sake, of course. How are you?"

"Knock off the sarcasm."

"Love the new heels," said the reflection.

"Aren't they divine? I have nothing to go with them."

"So I see. What's the occasion today?"

"Saving the damned, the usual."

"Oh, aren't you the busy bee."

"You know, you're right."

"About what?"

"Not having a thing to wear."

"You brought that one up. But you're correct. It's not right. You've spent your life in mortal combat with the evils and temptations of this world and this is the thanks you get? Empty closets? Nothing to wear?"

"What's a girl to do?"

A bright idea presented itself and he stopped plucking.

"Have a Special Collection."

"Of course, the poor slobs in, ah..."

"New Delhi."

"New Delhi?"

"Why not?"

"The Philippines. It sounds better."

"You're right, by God. The Philippines it is."

There was a knock at the door. From outside came a soft voice. "Father, it's two o'clock."

"Got to go," he whispered and winked into the mirror.

"Thank you, Sister," he replied sarcastically as he kicked off the heels. He pulled a girdle from his briefcase and struggled into it. "Mercy, this thing is shrinking by the minute. What's a girl to do?"

"I told you, have a Special Collection for a few new things. That's what a girl would do."

"You're brilliant, just brilliant."

The priest quickly donned his vestments, slipped into loafers, marched out the sacristy door to the confessional to hear the sins of the faithful for the next two hours.

Mercifully baseball was over for the day. It had temporarily lost its appeal, due partly to his grief and Joey's smart remarks, but mostly because of the big idea he'd had while idle in left. It had been floating around for awhile but now it was a plan. He went home, changed for confession and hit the sidewalk running. He ran all the way down the street.

He really was gonna go to confession this time, he really was. Reason one was to send up thanks that nobody had forced the altar boy issue today. Two was to say hi to his grandfather and he thought church was the place to do it, and three was this big idea. But first he had to run a thing or two by Professor Cromwell.

He arrived winded and excited.

"Hi Mrs. Cromwell, I'm Michael Kilgallen and Ray invited me over to look at his rockets."

Mike held Harriet's camera.

"Well, I'm delighted to meet you Michael. Raymond is in the garage. If you like, walk right around to the back. I'm sure he'll be happy to see you. Do you live nearby?" Mrs. Cromwell was the picture of Protestant conservatism.

"I live sixteen houses away. Right near the field. Ray showed us his gyroscope last summer in the rain."

"Oh. Oh, I see. Are you going to take pictures of Raymond's inventions?" she asked looking at Mike's camera.

Inventions? God knew what was in that garage. Space ships maybe.

"Ahm, I think so. I got it for my birthday and I wanted to show Ray," Mike lied.

"That's very kind, Michael. Go right around."

"Thank you, Mrs. Cromwell." Mike smiled.

Chapter 18

RAY WAS SEATED at a table covered with all sorts of gadgets and pieces of gadgets. There were little trays of nuts and bolts, screws, nails, and things that connected other things. Wires and tools and a torn apart TV were scattered everywhere.

"Hi, Ray," said Mike.

Ray turned around and smiled.

"Hey, Mike. Come on in. What's up? Holy cow, you came. Are you guys looking for a catcher or something?"

"Sure, but I got this really neat camera and I thought we could take some pictures of your rockets. If you want. Need any help or anything?"

Ray looked sad. "I can't make any rockets for awhile."

"How come?"

"Well I did the stupidest thing ever."

"What?"

"Well, I went down to the bridge before school on Friday 'cause I was gonna launch it there. 'Cause you can watch it for awhile before it begins to decelerate.

Can't light these things like firecrackers, you know. You have to detonate them from a distance. You know?"

"Kind of."

"Then the parachute activates so you can go get it and reload. If you can find it. If it doesn't get stuck in a tree. You know?"

Mike nodded right along.

"Wires, battery, a detonator. It takes time to set it all up. You know?"

"Yeah," Mike yawned.

"Everything's connected. You run the wires from the rocket to the firing mechanism. The base has to be a secure flat plane. Like this floor, flat. That's important. You aim it straight up, ninety degrees. Otherwise it's all guesswork. If it wobbles when it's fired..."

"So what happened? Did it work?"

"Well, yeah. But I got in trouble."

"Why?"

"Because I didn't detonate it at the bridge. I did it in my back yard but the base wasn't secure and, well... come on, I'll show you." They walked outside and Ray pointed up. "Weak base."

Sticking out of the next house, dangerously close to the bath room window, was the end of the rocket.

"Holy cow. It almost went through his house."

"It sure did. Weak base."

"What's all the black stuff around it?"

"Fuel burnout. And he isn't happy about it."

"Holy cow."

The neighbor was in the shower at seven AM when it hit. He was a veteran who'd seen action in France. In a flash he was on his driveway in a towel, caked in suds.

"Are you shitting me?" he'd screamed at Ray's father. "That crazy Nazi bastard scientist of yours nearly killed us. The war's over, facrisake. What is that kid, ten? Another four feet it would've gone right up my ass. Are you shitting me? They do this in Utah, facrisake. On mountaintops, away from people. God damn it. Look at my house. There's a rocket stuck in it, facrisake. Are you covered for rockets? I'm not covered for rockets. Ohhh, godddddamn it."

"That's what I mean by a solid base. They can fool you. They can go anywhere. You know?"

"Yeah, like the bathroom. Can I take a picture of it?" He didn't have a clue how to use the camera so he fumbled with it on purpose, which was part of the big idea he'd had in left field.

"That's a Polaroid. It's instant. All you do is aim and push that, and wait for a minute."

Mike aimed at the rocket stuck in the house and pushed the button but nothing happened.

Ray took it and popped open a little door. "You need film. What are you gonna use it for, a school project?"

"Kinda."

"What's the project?" asked Ray, in high interest.

"Flowers," Mike lied.

"Flowers?"

"Yeah."

"Just pictures of flowers? That's the project?"

"Well, it's just an idea."

"That's not gonna win anything. You're not over-coming any obstacles, or simplifying anything or... or anything."

"I know," Mike said sadly. "My grandfather died so I wanted to take pictures of his flowers before they died, too. He's got this big yard."

"Oh, jeez. Sorry, Mike. Tell you what, though. This thing isn't gonna work without film. It's empty, see?" Ray popped open the empty film carriage. "They sell it down the Square."

"Wanna walk down? We can get ice cream. I'll buy."

"Ice cream? Sure. I can bring my books back to the library, too. Don't forget the camera."

Ray's mother made him promise not to go near anything that flew or burned or exploded. Ray gave his word.

Not far away as the crow flies Gary and Creature were in the bathroom getting as handsome as nature would allow. Which wasn't a whole lot.

"How many chicks hang around this joint?" asked Gary.

A butt hung from the corner of his mouth. He was piling his hair as high as gravity permitted and giving his Rock Hudson grin a workout in the mirror. They were dressed in the usual getup of engineer boots, garrison belts, tee-shirts, dungarees and leather coats.

"Trust me. It's wall to wall chicks. You got money?" said Creature doing the same thing in the mirror.

"I got my money, yeah. You got your money?"

"Yeah, I got my money. Let's blow. The joint's filling up right now."

The joint was Daylight's Café in the Square. After confession it filled up with Irish and Italian high school girls pretending they weren't interested in the boys. And who could blame them. Half resembled an undead James Dean. Most of the rest, The King himself. For a nickel a song you could hear Elvis, the Everly's, Fabian, the Coasters, Johnny Cash and drink Coke until you exploded. Nearly every kid was a copy of some pop star. Looking for love and doing it badly.

The walk to the Square was another science lecture. This time Ray talked about lenses and cameras for Mike's edification. Galileo's name came up. And he, according to Ray, was the first guy to use a telescope to study the stars. And he got in trouble with the Pope for telling all his friends that the earth revolved around the sun. Again, Ray used a stick in the dirt to explain the phenomenon.

Mike wasn't feeling stupid this time. He asked a lot of questions and Ray answered them all. It was incredible. He knew everything. He said he never got a B on any report card he ever got. Mike thought to say, 'Hey, me either. Not even close.'

Ray pulled a compass from his pocket and began to explain that on the walk over the bridge.

They unloaded Ray's books at the library then went window shopping for bikes and model planes mostly. They spent a half hour in a hobby shop. Ray, as tour guide, knew every item and how to put it together. He bought the latest edition of Astounding Science Fiction magazine and read as he walked.

Gary and Creature hiked nearly a mile and a half in heavy boots and leather jackets on a warm June afternoon with the intention of displaying themselves in order to attract suitable females. As usual, neither gave a single thought to the dirt under their nails or the Oreo's stuck to their teeth.

They took the identical route which Mike and Ray had taken minutes earlier; down the hill, across the highway, over the bridge and then the short walk into the Square. Any adult citizen, upon seeing the pair, might have assumed that both were bound for alcoholism or prison. Or both.

The joke shop had every gag imaginable. All kinds of false teeth, all kinds of masks, rubber snakes, exploding cigars, anything.

"Put it there, pal, nice to meet ya." Ray held out his hand.

Mike shook it and got buzzed.

Mike bought himself a pair of Groucho Marx glasses, and two Frankenstein masks one for Ray.

"Hold this, will ya."

Ray took the camera and Mike put on his glasses. Ray laughed his ass off.

So did some lady with her two kids. One started crying because he wanted a pair of the same glasses. So his mother bought a pair, put them on the kid, and he shut right up. But the mother and older brother had laughed so hard the kid started crying again.

Outside they donned their masks and within minutes Groucho and Frankenstein had successfully snuck up on, and scared the shit out of four young Sandra Dee clones.

They walked by Brennan's Tavern. The door was wide open. They backed up. A bunch of guys sat around tables guzzling beer. With Frankenstein to his left Groucho stepped in and hollered with excellent intention, "Hey, you bums, who the hell's in charge here?"

All the patrons pointed to each other, laughing.

"We want a couple of hi-balls and a meatloaf sandwich," Groucho yelled.

The skit got a nine on the laughometer. One of the guys faked a chase so the kids took off.

"Well," the burly barkeep snickered, "I'm glad somebody around here knows what the hell it is they want."

Next was a beauty salon. Groucho and Frankenstein walked in like they owned it. Against each wall sat a dozen old ladies under hair dryers curling their white heads.

The little monsters waved to the girls and then screamed at the top of their lungs, "Caaaall for Philip Mooorrrrriiiiiiis," scaring the bejeezuz out of the beauticians and those customers with any hearing left.

Comments like "Oh, those little bastards. What's the world coming to? Tan their little hides," followed as they bolted out and laughed all the way to the next stop.

Which was the same ice cream parlor where Mike had overdone it the week before. They bellied up and ordered. Not until the order was completed, paid for and they'd taken their seats, did the masks come off.

Winded and sweating, the two Hell's Angels wannabe's arrived at Daylights. This was Saturday after confession, not Friday after school where there would've been a sea of female faces. But there were enough. Music from the juke box was non-stop and on every table sat a half dozen Cokes. The girls gabbed, giggled and sang along with hit tunes. They worked very hard to create the illusion of ignoring the boys.

A girl, pretending disinterest, will go to amazing lengths to display her assets. How she walks, how she sits or stands, leans to a friend to chat, or the manner in which she turns a corner in school with an arm full of books, all have purpose. The hair, the smile, hips, ass and boobs, all work in perfect harmony to communicate. Every single movement, calculated to attract. It's the dinner bell. All a guy has to do is swallow the bait, look her in the eyes, smile and offer to buy her a Coke. That's it. It's there for the taking. Millions of years of evolution guarantees it. All you need is a little nerve. But who's that cool at fourteen? Certainly not Creature or Gary.

Wendy spotted Creature and nearly gagged. She whispered to the girl opposite her in the booth and they traded places by climbing under the table. With her back to Creature she could breathe easier but her afternoon was ruined.

If anyone even suspected she'd swapped spit with that lunatic she'd just die. With her stomach in knots she prayed he would evaporate.

Naturally, Gloria, the girl she'd traded seats with, desperately needed to know which guy she was avoiding and why. Now Wendy had a pair of problems. Not to mention withholding her impure actions in confession an hour earlier.

They talked like tiny professors. Ray took out his compass. "It's pointed north. See?" The needle was on E.

"But the dial's on E," said Mike.

"You mean the needle's on E. Watch."

With a wry grin Ray turned the compass so the needle was on N. Mike looked stumped.

"It's one of those things. Every compass does it. If there were fifty on the table the needles would all point the same way, north. No matter what the dial said."

He took a pencil from his pocket and pointed.

"This is the needle and that's the dial. There're dials on phones, radios, clocks, scales..."

"Scales. My mother's always on ours."

"Mine, too. Watch this. The needle's pointing north. Right?"

Mike nodded. Ray turned the compass a couple of times until the needle was again on N.

"So South is that way. Right?" He pointed in the exact opposite direction.

Mike nodded, hung on every word.

"Ohhhhh!!! I get it. So east is that way. My house is that way. North. The field is... what's NE?"

"North East," said Ray.

"So from right here the field is North-East, right?"

"North, North-East. And if it goes over that dot the direction becomes East, North-East."

"Oh. Okay," said Mike, now genuinely interested.

"So where's the library?" asked Ray.

"Ah, wait a sec. Ahmm, West, South-West?"

"Correct."

"Jeez!" Suddenly it was a brand new world.

"You're good, Mike."

Ray cupped his hands around his mouth. "Pilot to co-pilot. Need a bearing on the coffee ice cream. Over."

Mike lined up the freezer and cupped his hands over his mouth. "Coffee ice cream. West, South-West, over."

"Roger that. Bald guy in the corner. Over."

"Bald guy, ah... east, south-east. Over."

"Roger. Need a bearing on the barber shop. Over."

Mike adjusted to the big window. "Barber shop. Exactly west. Over."

"Roger. Pilot to co-pilot. Open bomb bay doors. Over."

Mike pushed an imaginary button. "Bomb bay doors open. Over."

"Let her rip," said Ray.

Mike pushed another button and whistled as the payload dropped to earth below.

"Direct hit on my school with fifty tons of melted marshmallow. Mission accomplished. Over."

"Roger, direct hit with melted marshmallow."

Mike lined up more stuff. "So the vanilla is West of the chocolate. The nuts are East of the hot fudge."

"Nice work. When I'm big I'm gonna build a real rocket, you know? Did you see, 'The Day the Earth Stood Still'?"

"Oh, yeah. Wicked pissa. The spaceman was really a nice guy and then we shot him. And the robot was his best friend. His name was Gort. A kid was in it, too. I saw it at my grandfather's house. He let me stay up real late."

"Remember the rocket they landed in?" Ray asked.

"Yeah"

"Well, I can build one just like it."

"In your garage?"

"Maybe. After the guy's house is fixed."

Mike imagined all the kids dragging a fifty foot rocket from Ray's garage up the street on a couple of wagons.

"We could fire it off at the field. How much would it cost?"

"More than a hundred dollars."

Mike figured with his cash and a few more bucks they could be on Mars before the next altar boy lesson.

For two hours Creature and Gary stood like cardboard cutouts of motorcycle maniac, Marlon Brando in 'The Wild One'. Not one syllable was exchanged between them or with anyone else. They were discouraged and pissed off. And now the place was nearly empty. All the girls had walked right by the both of them as if they were invisible.

Gloria got bored and had threatened to leave so Wendy had to admit who she was avoiding or be left alone in the booth.

She told the gory story of the day in the woods with Creature. About him feeling her up (which she immediately regretted) and the puking kid who couldn't get his pants up, and Creature trying to kill the kid and then falling in the puke.

Gloria hung on every word, laughing or grimacing sourly, and Wendy made her promise not to tell a living soul. Especially the getting felt up part.

Poor Wendy, a train wreck at fourteen.

Finally, without a single hit between them, Creature and Gary walked from Daylight's Café. Gloria delivered the good news. Wendy sighed great relief and made promises to herself about men. They waited for another five minutes just to be safe. Besides, they didn't want to waste the rest of their fifth Coke.

Chapter 19

GARY LOVED PINBALL but Creature did not. After a few minutes of watching, Creature left Gary with his game and started home alone. The walk was slow and steamy. He crossed the bridge, the highway, got to the bottom of the hill, looked up and didn't like what he saw, so he sat on a wall to catch his breath. He squashed the ants he saw and tried to kill a bird with a rock but it missed by a mile. Bored, he started off again but stopped abruptly. He decided to walk the few yards to the traffic light and try hitching a ride on the highway to the other side of the hill. He'd done it before. That way he could avoid the walk up, over and down the other side of the hill to his house.

Within minutes the black car rolled to a stop.

Before the trek home they stopped to get film. Ray spoke with a clerk to be sure it was the right stuff. Satisfied, Mike bought two packs and off they went. His big idea from left field was to somehow take a picture of the priest in his high heels, blonde wig and exposed dick, then blackmail him out of his life.

He'd set it all up for the next altar boy lesson, and this was the part that made him real nervous; at just the right moment he had to produce the camera, snap the picture, yell 'Ha, ha, ha. I got you now' and jump out the window, where his bike would be waiting below. Just like Jimmy Olsen would do. He wouldn't stop peddling until he got home.

When he arrived at church next Saturday morning he'd have the camera concealed in his book bag. If asked about the book bag he'd say he was going over to his aunt's house and she was going to help him with his homework, because she was an ace with arithmetic and spelling. If asked about the lump in the bag, which was really the camera, he'd just say it was his baseball glove and a ball.

This was the big idea he'd conceived in left field. He'd gone over it and over it, and didn't see how this plan would be any more difficult than launching a space ship from second base with Ray.

"So, my leetle friend, why are your knees shaking so?" a wise and friendly voice in his head asked with a Spanish accent. It was the Cisco Kid's partner, Pancho.

At the top of the hill near Ray's house Mike suggested they walk to the field to take pictures of a possible launch site for the rocket.

In reality Mike's big idea was beginning to fester. He was unable to halt the dissolving images of shock on the priest's face when he snapped the picture, his daring leap from the window to his bike below, and the exquisite emotion of final triumph as he peddled away.

Ray's company, he figured, might keep him from eating the entire idea alive. He wanted to try out the camera but Ray didn't want to walk up to the field. Instead he suggested Mike take one of the rocket stuck in the house. Mike did, it came out fine, and the two kids said so long.

On the walk home he began to manufacture lies of his whereabouts. Oh yeah, he'd been to confession all right, and oh yeah, his penance was two Our Father's and two Hail Mary's. Anything more than that and there'd be questions at home. Was he stealing candy, was he breaking windows or throwing rocks at busses. He'd learned that lesson well enough.

The month before, after church on a beautiful Sunday morning in May, Mike and company had trespassed onto private property, the Johnson Estate. They'd climbed the fence, found the pool, stripped naked and dove in.

The place was spectacular. You could get lost, it was so big. Frankie actually did. He went wandering and got lost in a huge maze of perfectly manicured hedges. He wandered around naked for ten minutes before somebody heard him crying.

A little while later the caretaker showed up with a German Shepherd on a leash. They had only seconds to get out of the pool, gather clothes and start running while the dog barked and the caretaker screamed psychotic in Italian.

All nine made the mad naked dash from the pool, past the main residence, across the huge front lawn, out the front gate, making a hard right onto the rocky dirt road. That lead to a street busy with church traffic, which they crossed to get to another dirt road which brought them finally into the woods where they frantically got dressed.

Joey's cousin, Davey, had tagged along and he'd left his best pants, neatly folded, on a lawn chair by the pool. He walked home all alone in his shirt, shoes and underpants.

Anyway, Mike confessed all of it the next week and got the whole fucking Rosary as penance. The priest was livid and wanted his name, and his father's name. Mike offered up 'Robert Murphy', son of the same, terrified the episode would escalate into something his father might find out about. His mother asked what his penance was and stupidly he told her. And for days, there was the constant whine of "Why, why, why? For God's sake, why? Why the entire Rosary?"

There was a picture of a naked woman taped to the dashboard. She was lying seductively on a couch smiling at Creature. The priest said there were magazines with even better pictures in the back seat. Creature wasted no time. In short order the priest held out a pint. Would he like a drink before he was introduced to the girl in the picture? Creature blinked twice and dropped his jaw. Oh yes, she lived close by. There'd be an orgy that night and he was most invited. The girls, he said, were always looking for fresh young studs. Creature took the bottle.

Mike wasn't that hungry so was in no particular hurry to get home. He walked slowly while reading the box of film. There were ten to a pack. When one was left a red light went on. He juggled the camera, the bag containing the masks and the other box of film while reading.

Reaching the empty field he imagined all the kids gathered to watch the big launch. With some luck and a few more bucks he and Ray would soon be off to Mars. First things first, though.

Something moved over by first base near the tree line. Holy smoke, a baby deer eating grass. He'd never seen one before. It was tiny. He tip-toed up the road to the path, circled around the trees for a better view and got within a hundred feet. Capturing and taming it crossed his mind. That'd be too cool. Nobody would know. He'd keep it in the garage and play with it after school. What a neat thing to have, your own deer.

It was gone. Just like that. His attention had wandered and during that lapse the deer had melted into the woods. He went to the spot anyway but found nothing. Oh well. He decided to take some pictures and the dam seemed like the perfect place. And it just might yield a frog or two.

They were many minutes past Creature's stop. On the road to nowhere, as it were. Creature held the bottle in one hand and a dirty magazine in the other.

The priest introduced himself as 'Howie' and inquired about Creature's destination. Though occupied, Creature mumbled something about having no plans, so 'Howie' suggested they keep each other company, on the road to nowhere, until the orgy started. There was no shortage of booze and magazines, he said. There was even a dirty movie in the trunk of his car. He reached over and felt Creature's crotch and got no resistance.

The stream by first base broke sharply right and ran a hundred yards further into the woods. One day the previous summer Mike's gang had built a dam at the base of a big tree. A pretty good one, too. The exposed roots had helped to capture water and gave the dam a sort of fantasy charm. Now there was a small pool attracting an array of critters, and every so often the kids would wander over to check on the wildlife.

He shot the pool. The camera whirred, the film ejected, he counted to sixty then yanked the covering from the film. The image contained leaves, ripples on the water, shadows, rocks and...hey!

On the ground, a foot from the water was a turtle, the size of a quarter, overturned with all four feet paddling thin air trying to right itself. He turned the little guy onto its stomach and watched it make its way hurriedly into the clear pool. It swam to the rocks below.

Something else took to the water to his left. He didn't look, but once again his attention wavered for just that split second, and now the turtle too had somehow vanished before his very eyes. Pretty slick trick, he thought as he smiled into the pool.

Creature and the priest had pulled into the driveway beside the sad gray house, whose windows held hardly a shard of glass in its panes, having been a favorite target of Mike and company the last two summers.

Under the magazine which Creature held was the priest, blonde wig spread over Creature's lap. The priest came up for air, reassured a now groggy Creature the orgy was still on, and the girls would be arriving soon.

Mike put on his Groucho glasses and snapped a picture of himself. Glasses and all he followed the stream lazily looking for critters until it came to an end, disappearing into a pipe under a dirt road.

He saw a rabbit, a million squirrels but no sign of the little deer. Maybe it lived up by the old gray house? What the hell, he wasn't that hungry yet, he'd toss rocks at windows.

His big idea from left field was beginning to have the same ring as a history test he knew he would fail.

He tried not to think about failure as he collected rocks from the road and headed for the old gray house.

Beside the driveway was an inclined stone wall that ran from the dirt road, the length of the driveway, to the back of the garage, and nearly roof height. You could walk the wall and jump to the roof of the garage and peg rocks at the top windows in the house. There were no neighbors for hundreds of yards in any direction. Seeds of all sorts had taken root beside the foundation, under the porches, the surrounding yards, and the driveway. The hodge-podge of vegetation, it seemed, had a mind of its own, free to consume any trace of lingering memories, good or bad.

Something terrible indeed had stained the house forty years before. A handsome young man had gone off to Europe to fight The Great War. In that very house lived the love of his life, the only child of a doctor and his wife. They'd secretly married the day before his departure. Though wounded he'd survived, yet brought home the Influenza which killed tens of millions around the world in 1918. Shortly she succumbed to the disease as did her mother. The father, though a doctor, was powerless to save either one. He died of a broken heart on a chair in his daughter's bedroom on Christmas day the same year. The young man left his parents home and was never heard from again. It seemed, by the condition of the house, as if the ghosts of the players in this tragedy had been hard at work erasing a terrible memory.

Chapter 20

THE SIGHT OF the black car parked in front of the garage took his breath away. It was nearly hidden by tall weeds devouring the driveway. He shivered, ducked to the front of the house, trotted around the side, then to the back yard thick with growth. Someone sat on the passenger side. He had no doubts about the activities in the car. Mike shook as he took the camera from his bag.

His big idea from left field had given birth, materialized before his very eyes, and it stunned him. 'When you wish upon a star', the jingle by Jiminy Crickett was his first thought. His second was — you must be kidding — so attuned was he to getting exactly what he didn't want that it took a blinkless minute for it all to sink in.

It was show time. This was it. Such an opportunity might never again present itself but his feet wouldn't move. All he had to do was push a button. Walk a few feet and push a button. He knew what was going on, something unspeakable, but if he spooked whoever it was they might run him down and beat the crap out of him, or much worse.

This wasn't a squabble in the schoolyard with a bully. This was the real deal. In that car, twenty feet away, was the object of his nightmares. In his shaking hands he held the power to change the course of his own future. His mind clouded and his legs went soft. His fear was overwhelming. Settling for a life of slavery under control of the priest suddenly seemed agreeable, even logical and comforting.

That thought he realized, the idea of doing nothing to defend himself, was what made him shake, not his duty ahead. But unlike any fight in the woods, losing here, getting caught here, meant consequences too terrible to ponder. He inched closer to the car, camera at the ready.

The telephone rang, much too loud for Wendy's fragile nerves. The poor kid had been through hell these last few hours and her thoughts were too horrible for words. What if Creature had blabbed about feeling her up? What if every boy in school knew? What if her name and phone number were scrawled above every urinal in town? 'For a good time call Wendy.' 'Wendy goes down.' God Almighty! How did she get sucked in by that demented freak. If only she'd confessed it when she had the chance. She only went to Daylights because she felt guilty about the bad confession. And now Gloria knew and... Gloria seemed okay. But she knew how some girls talked. Oh God! Creature! She could kill him.

Her mother yelled from downstairs. She rose heavily from her bed and went to the top of the stairs.

"What?!" poor Wendy screamed..

"Do you want to baby sit tonight? And don't you talk to me in that tone of voice, little lady."

"For who?"

"What do you care for who? It's fifty cents an hour. It's a ten minute walk. That's who," her mother screamed back.

"Okay!!!"

Willie Mays spoke as plain as day.

"Say hey, Mike. Got yourself in a rundown I see. You leaned too far off second, that's all, kid. You committed. But I gotta tell you, this ain't no series in April where it don't matter a whole hell of a lot. This here's the Fall Classic, Mike. And these guys are good. They'll come after you. Know what I mean?"

"Yeah."

"But I seen you run, kid. You can fly. Some day we'll play ball. You, me and the guys. Okay?" said Willie kindly.

"Okay."

"Mike?"

"Yeah?"

"You got to do the right thing here."

"Yeah, but..."

"It ain't popular and it ain't democratic, the right thing. Sometimes you're all on your own. Got to be done all alone. No help from nobody."

"Willie?"

"Yeah, Mike."

"I'm afraid."

"I know. Believe me, I know. So was I. Ain't kiddin' neither. Mighty scared. Oh, yeah. I can tell stories. Man I got stories. Tell you 'bout Jackie sometime, too."

"Oh, jeez, Willie."

"Ain't never easy, Mike. You keep your eye on that ball. You do what's right. Make it a game."

"Willie...?

"Do it now. While I'm right here."

"But..."

"Do it now, Mike."

He stood and swallowed nervously. He checked his Groucho glasses and moved slowly through the tall weeds to the car. Crouching low he crawled around the back of the car and wedged his way silently between the stone wall and the passenger side. The window was open. He raised the camera. Not knowing what to say or do or feel he knocked on the small fly window.

"E...excuse me," he said politely. A glassy eyed Creature looked into the camera holding a pint of Wild Turkey and a dirty magazine. The priest looked up from Creature's lap into the camera, holding Creature's dick in his hand. Mike pressed the button.

"Jesus God!" screamed the priest. "Jeez, Chri... hey you get...get back here... oh, Jesus God above."

Mike side stepped between car and wall, ran for his very life down the driveway, across the dirt road and into the woods.

The priest threw his long blonde hair in the back seat and started the car.

Running madly for the safety of the woods he heard the car scream into reverse. Down the driveway to the dirt road, it rocketed. The sound of spinning tires grinding through dirt and stone was as thick in the air as Mike's imagination. The car was coming after him, driving through the woods to run him down. Impossible, but true. Despite the obstacles of trees, bushes and boulders, it gained.

Behind the wheel the priest had transformed into a smiling skeleton. Blood flowed from horns on its skull, into empty black eye sockets. From the grill dozens of long whirling razor sharp blades shredded everything in its path. It cackled wildly at its prey's impending demise.

Mike's knees went gimpy and he screamed aloud. He ran for his life, lungs on fire. He detoured further into the woods to shake what was following. But the roaring engine and grinding wheels were nearly upon him now, coming through the trees, turning everything in its wake into hot coals.

He heard the screaming skull, a yard behind his own. He fell to the ground, waiting to be sliced and diced into a warm stew.

The car was speeding away, its din of engine and shifting gears dissipating in the distance.

He struggled for air, tried to stand but his legs refused. His regret was mounting. Oh, boy. He'd done it this time. He'd really done it this time. Why? Whatever had possessed him? He must've been out of his mind

At least he'd held fast to his bag of goods, he thought, as he tossed in the Groucho glasses. He gazed at the film protruding from the camera, now merely a symbol of his own stupidity. He entertained the idea of tossing the lot in with the turtle, wishing the last ten minutes of his life could be relived, realizing sadly the picture probably didn't mean shit.

He was crying, exhausted, terrified and alone. All alone in a world numb to his desperate fight to keep his soul intact. Alone in a world oblivious to his struggle to obey God's natural law and the teachings of Christ Himself, blind to a young boy's lonely crusade to prevent Satan from stealing his soul and taking it to hell.

And what did he think he was he gonna do with a time bomb like this? Pedal over to The Daily Planet and hand it over to Perry White?

"Grrrrate Caesar's ghost, young man. Why... why, is this what I think it is? Run down the hall and deliver it to Louis Lane, would you? She'll turn it over to Super Man and he'll deal with it. Don't you worry about a thing, my boy. Now get going. Great Caesar's ghost."

It probably wouldn't phase the priest in the slightest. His imagination quieted somewhat as his breathing normalized. Sadly he realized, he wasn't Jimmy Olsen after all.

It was pandemonium. The priest drove like a psycho wheel man after a bank job. Creature, drunk as a skunk, bobbed around the front seat as the priest whipped the car into right turns and left turns, heading for the hills.

"Was that Gowsho Maas, Howie?" Creature slurred. Were they on their way to the orgy? Would the lady on the dashboard really, really be there? He pointed to the picture and fell forward bonking his head on the steel dash.

The priest moaned psychotically as he drove, oblivious to Creature's ramblings. Get rid of this pile of shit, he told himself. Dump it. Kick it out. He was still driving erratically, still shaking from the shock. If that kid... Jesus, that kid! Where in the world had he come from? He slowed the car.

He was miles away but the kid had a picture, a very scary scenario. The chance of it being seen by anyone was slight. But the slightest chance in this case could not be tolerated. He knew, over the years, the last thirty, that none had uttered a word to a living soul. Their utter humiliation and terror was his ace in the hole.

He suspected, in this boy's case, it was a matter of holding a tiger by the tail. At least he hoped that was the case. Still, he was a very worried woman, in that there was always the slim chance that one of them one day would fight back. And with proof like that it would not be much of a fight.

Little by little his strength was returning. Still, his legs felt like spaghetti. Shaky spaghetti. He was squatted on the big root next to the dam, dirty, sweaty and weak, recreating an afternoon that never happened. Wishing he'd gone to confession and not to Ray's, wishing he was just getting out of bed, the day just beginning. Wishing this and wishing that, pissed off at Willie and himself. Certainly there could have been a better way, a more comforting solution.

He'd opened a can of worms which now could never be shut. The sleeping giant had awakened, hungry. And it ate little boys. Surely the priest knew it was him. Surely this was way beyond a beating with a belt. It was up there with excommunication and reform school, or worse. He was now toe to toe with the worst possible enemy. Me and my bright ideas, he thought.

In deep thought Wendy looked at her reflection. She might clear five bucks. That'd buy her some new duds. Maybe that's what attracted that creep in the first place, her choice of fashion.

Maybe she'd get a new set of friends, too. Taller, smarter, friendlier, like Annette and Bobby on Mickey

Mouse. She doubted their mother's bitched about other people when they weren't around, nor, she thought, did they seem the type to yell and scream. They were from California. All smiles and warm hearts. The Creature thing was killing her. She decided, then and there, to become an actress. But which one?

He was starving. The moment had arrived to leave the woods and go home. So, he was late. Fuck it. He and Ray were calculating a top secret manned mission to moon. No. Ray had helped him with his arithmetic. They'd have to settle for that. He'd offer no more. He was in no mood for any shit from anyone. It was the second worst day of his life and tomorrow he had church to look forward to, and with his luck it'd be Devlin on the altar.

He stood and checked his bag. At the sight of the camera he nearly choked. He extracted the film and stuffed both in the bag. In it was the camera, the Groucho glasses, the Frankenstein mask, the remaining pack of film. And the time bomb. He had roughly eighty bucks in his back pocket.

He took his usual route home, out of the woods, across the field, across the road, across two back yards and hid the bag in his next door neighbor's garage. The back window was broken and there was a shelf inside within easy reach. He hid his Halloween candy there one time.

He then dashed through a few more back yards, up a driveway, onto the street and doubled-back toward his house. There were several cars parked in front. Good news.

The booze would be running with everyone as happy as larks. His lies of his whereabouts would hold up because nobody would really care or cross examine. Even if they did bother to ask.

"Here he is, now. Cardinal K, what's the good word, my son?" his high-ball sipping father joked.

All laughed. There was a room full of people dressed up, ready to hoot and holler. His sisters wandered like sheep in a field of giraffes. Mike went for the kitchen.

His mother appeared with a smile, a high-ball and a flushed face.

"We're going out to eat. The baby sitter will be here in a second. So behave. Look at you. You're a mess. You missed dinner again, for God sake," she shrieked. "You'll look like a damn refugee."

Mike ignored her and spooned goulash into his face from a pan.

"Did you go to confession? Who'd you get? Who'd you go with? What was your penance?"

Before he could answer his uncle Pete, the engineer, came in to collect Mrs. K.

"Baby sitter's here, Claire." To Mike, he said, "Hey, big guy, how's it going? Taking altar boy lessons I hear. Boy that's something."

Mike nodded as he chewed. Mrs. K's mood turned from Grand Inquisitor to smiling parent, proudly displaying her first experiment.

"I hear Father D took a shine to you. That can't hurt. Says you're headed for the big time in the Vatican. Well, let me tell ya, we're all gonna need somebody inside one of these days, if you know what I mean. Right, Claire?" he chuckled as he held up his glass.

"Come on, we're leaving. Oh, Wendy. Damn it. Is she waiting?" said Mrs. K as she raced from the room.

Wendy. Wendy? Wendy from the woods? Mike went stiff and stopped chewing.

The priest dragged Creature from the car and left him for dead behind a paper mill, beside the river, miles from home. Creature had stumbled from the loading dock, through the parking lot to the road, trying to solve his location. Someone had called the cops.

Being totally shitfaced, gripping the empty pint in one hand and a dirty magazine in the other, did not prevent Creature from trying to convince the cops that this was not what it appeared to be. The cops tossed the bottle, took the magazine, dumped him in the back of the meat-wagon, and took off.

Mike yanked the Frankenstein mask from his bag in the neighbor's garage and put it on. Wendy! He'd never been more humiliated in his life. And now this. What a day.

A gloomy Wendy sat in a chair paging through Look Magazine. Mike's sisters ran around like little lunatics screeching and fighting. She was in no mood for this. No mood for anything but peace and quiet. Her thoughts were of that asshole Creature when she felt a presence.

She turned and shrieked. Frankenstein himself stood in the hall at the foot of the stairs. He looked at her a long moment and then headed up.

"God Almighty! Who are you?" she demanded, following him to the foot of the steps.

Mike kept walking.

"Is that your brother?" she asked of the two older sisters as the door to his room slammed shut.

"Yup," one of them said without looking from the TV. "But don't smell his finger."

They both giggled.

Chapter 21

FATHER McAULEY WAS happy to fill in. The priest was not quite up to it this morning. Though he thought it odd, at the last moment to be asked the favor, he said nothing. Although there was strained communication between the two, he offered his help with his usual understanding smile,. Father McAuley had once tried to confide in Devlin. A period of heavy doubt concerning his faith had plagued him for many weeks.

Father McAuley was a ball of positive energy, always smiling, always helping, always on the go. He'd assembled an orchestra made up of a dozen kids with the help of a music teacher from the parish. He'd put together basketball teams, softball teams, and a golf team. He'd organized school dances in the hall beneath the church. Nothing made him happier than happy groups of people. The more happiness he saw, the more he wanted. No one on God's green earth was happier with his calling.

But with each attempt to create a sense of congregation within the parish he was balked. Ultimately, meeting failure with every attempt. Unknown to him, like a soldier in a sniper's sights, were Devlin's efforts to destroy it all.

At the height of his desperation, at his wits end, he'd approached Devlin and asked for his counsel. It was one of the strangest moments of his life. There fell a long silence. Devlin's eyes seemed to cloud over, with no acknowledgement whatsoever that he'd even heard Father McAuley's cry for help. He'd never forgotten the strange expression on Devlin's face.

He'd have sworn before Almighty God Himself on Judgment Day that what he saw was a faint smile cross the priest's lips, and what he perceived was immense joy within the priest upon seeing another's suffering.

Yes, Father McAuley was delighted to fill in. Though he loved to say mass, read the Epistles, recite his Gospels, he was equally delighted to be as far from Devlin as he could get. On more than several occasions he'd endured the priest's terrible crushing silence while in the same room. And no, it was not his imagination.

The priest was a worry wart to the tenth power. How on earth was he to get his hands on this damnable evidence? How? Would there be a surprise today? He'd heard a horrible tale of two such incidents years ago.

In New York state a boy had informed his father of an incident which took place during a church camping trip.

The priest and a counselor were abusing the boys. It apparently had been going on for years.

"He just seemed so quiet and unhappy after the trips. We thought it was the water or the food or something. But the doctor found nothing wrong," one mother was heard to say. *"I'm having a very hard time with this. I still can't believe it happened in our church."*

Someone had looked into it. Someone had acted. The priest and one of the counselors had to answer questions. Word had gotten out but it was contained in the nick of time. That cost the church an arm and a leg.

But before that had nearly sneaked out of the closet and into the headlines there was an incident in Chicago. The father of a courageous young boy had let it all hang out to a full house on Easter Sunday.

In the middle of the Gospel he stood, marched from his pew, up the aisle, onto the altar to within a yard of the guilty priest and screamed as loudly as he could.

"If I see you on the street, if you come within a thousand feet of my son I will fuck you to death with the rusty axle on my pick-up truck. I know who you are and I know what you've done."

He was quieted by several other men, but none in the church had missed a single word. Yet again the offender was simply moved to another parish. Not a newspaper in the state, not a single public official pursued the incident. In fact several had acquired new lakeside homes. And the priest was left free to continue a poisonous rampage of innocent children.

This is what occupied the mind of the priest this Sunday morning. He paced the living room of the rectory, certain that soon the walls would come crashing in, followed by police brandishing handcuffs and straightjacket with guns drawn. With screaming parents and young victims gathered on the lawn to hail justice being served.

He was aware of two suicides due to his actions, and a slew more turned destitute, crazy and alcoholic.

None of the usual mechanisms, none of the identities or justifications which had served so splendidly to override his heinous existence, were coming to his aid this morning. The crimes he would one day answer for, one day be judged for, were coming to life in a dull purple-gray shimmer.

Oozing into focus from the furniture, carpet, ceiling, and walls were faces of his young victims staring squarely at him through sad, defeated eyes. He moaned aloud and ran for the liquor cabinet.

The Body and Blood of Christ was being administered as it had for a millennium. It was a beautiful morning to give praise and to recognize the awesome power and goodness of the Supreme Being. And maybe ask a favor. Everyone seemed at peace. Everyone looked to be residents of ideal havens; soft spoken, pipe smoking fathers, and smiling, cookie baking, squeaky clean mothers with quiet, well behaved and studious children.

Everyone seemed content. Maybe it was the glorious spring sunshine. Maybe it was the young and energetic Father McAuley on the altar. Maybe it was Ike at the helm in the Oval Office holding off the commies. But Mike felt happy for them all. It was how the world should be.

Regardless of whether yesterday's adventure was a mortal sin, or a crime against humanity, or both, he was going up. Father McAuley was on the altar, so no sweat. He liked Father McAuley. He needed a lift and besides, his grandfather might be watching and all kinds of shit was going through his mind.

He felt heavy and wooden. He'd awakened sometime in the early hours to a still house and had not slept since. Yesterday had lasted a week, and now he was exhausted and afraid. Yesterday, a priest, a Creature and a Wendy. More like the pages in a horror comic.

He didn't feel like talking with Willie or anybody else. It wouldn't help. Communion had helped a little. Upon returning to his pew he offered up a couple to his grandfather and tried not to think of his problems. It was a beautiful day and school would be out for the summer shortly, he reminded himself.

He took the long way home, past the wealthy estates with their long circular drives and huge shade trees. He walked past the Johnson estate with its magnificent gardens and pool. He longed to be inside, to feel safety and comfort and ownership. He imagined the happy adventures of exploring its attic, basement and its many rooms. His steps were heavy and slow. He thought of a place to sit and rest and soon arrived. He laid down and went fast to sleep.

The priest felt much better after a third of the bottle was gone, back on his toes, so to speak. He began to analyze and evaluate. First, he was a priest. That meant a lot of things to a lot of people, and not all of them completely rational. This he knew.

People stuttered and mumbled in his presence, became giddy and acted foolishly. To him they told their deepest and darkest secrets, or most of them. Which to them might mean that he was completely sinless. Which might mean he could read minds, raise the dead, talk to the dead, walk on water, fly at night, anything. They made it up. They manufactured the truth. This he knew, too. Their ignorance was his bliss. And it gave him the warm and fuzzies. He gazed confidently out the big picture window of the living room, planning and scheming.

There are two ways people ordinarily accept things, neither of them very good. One, accept a statement because Authority says it's true and must be accepted. Two, is by preponderance of agreement among other people, public opinion, the general test for sanity or insanity. The definition of sanity becomes then, whether or not a person agrees with everyone else. A very careless way of accepting evidence, but nearly always it is the primary measuring stick. For example...

Once upon a time the world was flat. True statement. It's only been a round ball for a thousand years or so. When it was flat people knew you fell off the edge if you sailed out too far; certain they were of strange occurrences like sailing into space, or horrible creatures like giant bats, seven headed sea serpents and psychiatrists. You name it. They knew it was there.

Possibly the first men to sail beyond the horizon were a couple of kids who, borrowing a boat, had sailed out of sight. Upon returning they excitedly told their friends of their excellent adventure, and the kids who heard the tale repeated it, and so on. Well, it's safe to assume somebody's mother found out and there was hell to pay. So the kids, who'd sailed beyond the horizon, observing only more water and no bats, found themselves in some trouble.

There'd be no more sailing for them. At least not until they learned, from Authority, and from everyone else, what was really over that horizon. Regardless of their discoveries and sincere pleas of "I can prove it" or "go see for yourself", they'd be walking not sailing, for some time.

Now, let's say the kids had nerve enough to re-experience their excellent adventure. Got the boat again, sailed over the horizon again, got back safely again. Got caught again. Only this time the witch doctor finds out.

He's the village shrink, the Authority figure, the guy in charge of spells, and what's true and what isn't. The right spell at the right time keeps the giant bats out of sight and him in business. So far he's done a marvelous job, nearly no complaints and very few bat sightings. He might be a nice guy, get a kick out of the whole thing, and hand the kids back to their mothers.

But let's say he's not a nice guy. Let's say he's nuts, terrified of losing his Authority and title. Because with title go perks. He's got the lock on all the virgins, and a slice of all the goods used for trade with other villages. Soon the sailing thing, with word of its new discoveries, gets very loud and out of hand and winds up in his lap. Now the witch doctor has a problem.

All know the world is flat and beyond the horizon are indescribable horrors. Giant bats, psychiatrists and so on. No question about it, everybody knows. But the kids say different. And people are talking. And he doesn't like hearing the 'I can prove it' shit, because in order to maintain his title he must act in accordance with 'the council of truth'.

The council being the guys who depend on the witch doctor to constantly fill the village mind with giant bats in order to maintain their control by fear. And they're the guys the witch doctor depends upon to keep his title, his perks, and his life.

So, the council's main job (and their slice of pie depends upon it) is keeping the witch doctor active in creating more and more giant bats. The whole package is wrapped in ribbons of fear. Fear among the council that too many people might set sail and discover for themselves they've been bamboozled. And fear in the boys that no one will believe them. The council's only hope is preponderance of agreement, a collective village mind chock full of giant bats and sea serpents.

If that fear begins to unravel then the council gets nervous. So the decision of whether the boys live or die becomes based on which way the wind is blowing that day. And the wind always blows in the right direction for them. They need only sober up the witch doctor, get him dressed, remind him of his crimes, and instruct him to deliver an eloquent expert opinion on the existence of giant bats, and the hopeless insanity of the kids, so that the matter is put to rest.

The boys are found guilty, put to death, and a law passes forbidding all villagers from gazing out at the horizon.

Welcome to planet earth. Everybody, back to work!

And the priest knew this. He'd been employing it for years as a means of cruising under the radar to carry on his criminal existence. He was a holy man with powerful friends. He could go anywhere and do anything with impunity. Yet all this might be in jeopardy. He continued to analyze.

Could this kid be from another parish? Could he be a Protestant kid or a Jew who happened to be in the woods at that time? He could not have been followed by this boy, he was driving a car. Kids don't drive to the woods. They walk because they live nearby. There was no rhyme nor reason in thinking it was anything but a fluke. A chance encounter. A kid in the woods with a mask. And a camera. A mask and a camera. A kid in the woods with those things was nothing out of the ordinary. Odd, yet it didn't have the ring of a planned operation. This is what kids did. And every so often they would stumble across other people in the woods. Near abandoned houses. In cars. Having sex. It happens.

But sneak up on other people at the most com-
promising moment imaginable and then capture it on
film? No, sir. This is not what little boys did. But some
little boy had. That this was planned was out of the
question. Impossible. He himself did not know he would
be there at that time.

For the life of him he could not arrange the factors into a sensible equation. But, several factors
occurring coincidentally in time and space? A kid in the
woods with a camera? Two people in a car parked by an
abandoned old house, near the woods? Without
question, a definite possibility. So it was a fluke. He'd
arrived at this conclusion in logical fashion. It satisfied
him for the moment. But what ate at his gut and
blurred his vision were the consequences of miscalcula-
tion. He took another belt of booze. He had no choice.
He had to go where logic led him.

Now, which kid with Groucho Marx glasses and
an instant camera lived in that neighborhood?

The priest decided to return to the scene, or at
least ride around the scene and think about it some
more. He dressed in short sleeve black shirt with collar
and, happy to be back in the game, went looking for
little boys who might be alone and have some answers.

Chapter 22

WHERE HAVE YOU been? For the love of God, what is it you think we do around here, your father and me? Do you think we run some kind of flop house or something? I mean for God's sake... the least you could do is show up once in a while. What the hell do you do all day out there, anyway? I can't imagine what your father has in mind for you when he gets back."

And to the High Heavens, "God Almighty, why can't that kid be normal? What the hell have I done with my cigarettes?"

Not "Are you okay, sweetie? Are you hungry? Sit down, I'll make you something." Just the same nerve shattering shit he'd been hearing for ten years. Amazing.

"Well?" she shrieked.

"I went over to Pop's. I sat under the apple trees and ate apples and fell asleep," he lied.

Maybe she'd start crying and shut up.

"Well, Rip Van Winkle, you can explain that one to your father. He's out looking all over town for you."

"Why?" Mike whined back.

"Why? Why? Because it's normal. That's why. And don't you use that tone with me. Don't you have homework or something to do for God sake? "

"School's almost over. There's no more homework."

Please God, don't remind her of the altar boy shit.

"As if you ever did any. Father Devlin said you had a ton of potential. Well I don't see an ounce of it. Now, get out of my sight."

And once more to the Heavens, "Why the hell can't that kid be normal?"

The baby began crying.

He walked worriedly out of the room. His father would be back shortly. God only knew what that meant.

An hour into his search and destroy mission the priest came upon two boys playing ball in the street. He parked the car got out and walked casually up the street then back toward his car. He held a prayer book for image.

"Hello, boys."

"Hello, Father," one of the boys said.

"Well, how are the Red Sox doing this year?"

The kids only shrugged and said "Okay, I guess."

Then one asked "Did someone die?"

"Heavens, no. I'm looking for a boy who has a camera."

"What's his name, Father?"

"Well, I was hoping someone could tell me because I wanted to borrow it and pay the boy a little money to use it. You see it's Sunday and ..."

The owner of the house behind him walked up his driveway into his front yard. He had car keys in one hand and his daughter in the other.

"Good afternoon, Father," the man said cheerfully. "What brings you to this neck of the woods?"

The priest did not recognize the man and felt momentarily flatfooted. Let's see, he thought, what am I doing here?

"Hello, I'm Father Devlin from Saint Catherine's. And getting expert advice on the Red Sox chances this year," he winked.

The man smiled.

"I'm John Doherty, Father. This is my daughter, Ellen. We go to St. Joseph's on the other side of town."

Little Ellen hid behind her father's legs. The boys had gathered to listen to the conversation.

"What a small world. I was in the seminary with Father McLaughlin. Of course, that was in the late eighteen hundreds. We talk often, he and I."

"Oh, no kidding. Father Mac's a great guy."

"Been at St. Joe's thirty years now. Does wonderful work. I just dropped off a carload of kids after mass. I need a camera for an hour, and one of them said his father had one, one of those instant camera's. Turns out he didn't. I'll just wait until the stores open tomorrow."

"Ray has one," one of the kids said. "But he's Protestant."

The two adults snickered.

"Oh well, I'm sure Ray's a fine student," said the priest winking to Mr. Doherty.

"He's a scientist, too. We saw him in the joke shop. Yesterday was my birthday. My mother got me a mask," the same kid said.

"Well happy birthday, my boy. Which mask did you get?"

"Clarabell. And he got glasses because he was crying," said the boy pointing to his younger brother.

The priest's interest peaked. "Glasses, you don't say," he said to the smaller one.

"Yes, Father. Funny one's." He yanked the Groucho glasses from a back pocket and put them on.

The priest laughed aloud. No one could imagine his surprise. He looked skyward and said nostalgically "Groucho Marx. Those were the days. Maybe my prayers have been answered, after all." He winked again at John Doherty who smiled right along.

It was all too easy.

"And Ray, you say, is a scientist?"

"Yes Father, he lives on the next street. The yellow house. Ray and his friend walked home with theirs on. Is that a sin?"

"Let's see now." He then paused a moment. "They walked home from the joke shop wearing masks. Is that a sin?" He frowned and rubbed his chin. "How many boys?"

"Just Ray and his friend, Father."

"Which masks did they wear?"

"Those," he pointed to his brother's glasses, "and a Frankenstein."

"And how old were they?"

"Ray's in fifth grade, Father."

"Hmm, no. I don't think that one's a sin. But with your masks on you have to be extra careful on the street for cars and busses."

"Yes, Father."

"Well, I wonder if the Protestants will help the Catholics today? No, I think I'll wait until tomorrow. John, it was my pleasure meeting you. And you too, Ellen. Isn't she adorable. You boys watch out for cars, and keep the faith, now. All of you."

He'd wait until dinner time to make his introduction to the mother of Ray the scientist.

It was Sunday. God damn it, everything was closed. The world shut down on Sunday. A nervous anxiety had filled the head of Mr. K as he drove home from his brother's house, where he'd borrowed a six pack. The wife had the curse and the kids were screaming. His thoughts were unpleasant. His eyes were narrowed and his lips shut tight. That God damn kid of his never listened. Nor, did the God damn kid ever do a thing he was told to do. He disappeared with the wind and couldn't be found. He had zero discipline and wasted all his time with those God damn morons at that field when he could be and should be in his room studying.

He and his bride had concluded that this morning, while nursing brutal hangovers. He'd see that his own mistakes weren't repeated. Indeed he would. He cursed himself for not borrowing half a case. His brother had two refrigerators, one for beer and it was always filled. He had to hand it to him, the fucking guy was always thinking ahead.

Too much wasted time, that was it. That God damn kid would spend the summer in his room, buried in books. The little bastard would get an education if it killed the both of them. What the hell was his problem? He never opened his God damn mouth at home. Who knew what he was thinking, or what he was up to all day long with those friends of his. He was Harry Houdini when it came to getting out of the house. By Jesus, the little bastard would find out who was boss under that roof the minute he got back to the house. Spare the rod, spoil the child. He heard that from somebody once and it sounded like good advice. The little moron was a perfect example. God damn it, that kid would get what was coming. He'd have to learn the hard way. But by God, he would learn.

The priest knocked and waited. He held a piece of paper for effect. A woman answered and he put on a puzzled face. She smiled, looking equally puzzled to see a priest at her doorstep.

"For heaven sake," he looked at the piece of paper "I must have taken the wrong turn. I was looking for the Doherty home."

"I think you may have, Father. They're nearly behind us on Highland Ave."

"This is happening far too often," he laughed.

"Well, thank you, Mrs...? I'm Father Devlin at St. Catherine's, over the hill."

"I'm Grace Cromwell, Father. I'm delighted," she said smiling pleasantly.

"Well, I'm sorry to bother," then he flashed his best perplexed expression. "Cromwell. Cromwell. Don't tell me Raymond is your boy."

Proudly surprised she said, "Well yes, how...?"

"Raymond is the envy of our best students. They say he's the brightest boy in town. MIT material, I'm told. A future scientist. I'm happy for you, Mrs. Cromwell."

"Oh, heavens, we had no idea. I don't know what to…"

"One of Raymond's admirers lives nearby, in fact." The priest chuckled. "Always taking pictures. What's the boy's name now? There I go again."

He chuckled and started to back down the steps.

"Oh, I know the boy, he was here yesterday. Michael. A nice boy. He's probably the boy you're referring to."

"My, my. What a small world."

"I asked if he lived nearby." She laughed at the thought. "He said he lived near the field, sixteen houses away. Not half a mile or a quarter, mind you, sixteen houses. And he was so cute with his camera. Ker? Cal?"

The priest snapped his fingers "Kilgallen."

"Of course, that was his name. Michael Kilgallen?"

"Of course, Michael, a delightful boy. Well, I'm glad to see he keeps good company. Again, pardon the intrusion, Mrs. Cromwell. And give my regards to your son, would you?"

"I'll do that. Have a nice evening, Father," she nodded pleasantly.

The priest walked back to his car with an evil ear to ear grin. The wheels began to spin. A plan was coming to life an inch behind his forehead.

Chapter 23

"OKAY. WHERE'D YOU get the booze, kid?" The cop asked, settling into his worn wooden chair. He was unsmiling in his short-sleeve shirt and tie. He had forearms like duck pins. His partner looked even less congenial like a snake ready to strike.

Creature looked as if he'd survived a mile long tumble down a ski trail in the Blue Hills, in July.

"What were you doing down by the paper mill completely shit faced at six o'clock on a Saturday?" asked Duckpin.

"Breaking and entering. We already know that," answered Snake.

"I got you down here as P. Latch. I'm guessing it's the same P. Latch that did a stretch last year at Deer Island for car theft. Your record's as long as my tie. Not fifteen and you've been inside," stated Duckpin.

"Attempted. I did ninety days. How'd you know my name," Creature managed.

"What do you think, we're stupid around here? Written on the inside of your jacket, tough guy," said Snake.

"Public intoxication, B&E will draw half a year from any judge. At least," said Duckpin.

"I never went into the mill."

"Where'd you get the half pint? I'm not asking again," said Duckpin.

At that point Snake took off his jacket and hat. He sized up Creature and began to pace like a boxer.

"You're going back to the Island until Christmas, tough guy. Now, what the fuck were you doing at the paper mill, who were you with, and where did you get that booze?" he demanded.

Creature was in every sense a passenger on the Titanic. He had three choices, all hopeless. Pray the sinking would stop. Jump into ice water. Or, tell the whole truth and nothing but. Tell them all about Howie with the black car? Right.

Oddly he wondered if he'd gone to that orgy, and then forgotten. Creature swallowed hard and licked his lips.

Tearfully he said, "I found it beside the river. Honest to God."

Meanwhile, back in the rectory the priest went for the bottle of scotch. He was excited that this matter would soon be concluded, and his life back to normal. Oh yes, it had been a most productive afternoon. His mental motor was humming.

He'd see to it that Mike's final report card would ensure he'd not be promoted and he'd spend the summer looking forward to another year with the Blade. He'd visit the Kilgallen residence and scare the shit out of the entire household. They'd have ulcers in a month. Needed only was a grim forecast of a life of crime, prison and a brief reminder that Judgment Day was not a day at Fenway.

He'd quote a passage or two for a nice touch. He'd weave a beauty. *Yes, of course I'm praying for Michael. Aren't we all? Believe me, Mrs. Kilgallen, no one occupies more of my thoughts these days.*

The parents wore the dull expressions of drinkers and TV watchers. They would agree to an exorcism if he so said. They, as did the rest, would believe anything. Hitler himself was fond of saying that the capacity to think had escaped the masses. He'd mold them as he saw fit. Yes, he'd have them all in knots.

He'd drive the kid crazy. He'd haunt that ball field. He'd stand beside his car and stare, like a wolf in sun glasses. He'd have the Blade phone the residence and convey her unhappiness over Mike's constant disturbances. Something must be done about it, she'd insist sternly. She'd place the call at dinner-time. That was always the best time. The father would not spare the belt. He'd turn the kid into a zombie. The priest would have them all in the palm of his hand. The boy would be his anytime he wanted.

There was a dozen ways of manipulating the parents into handing the kid over. They believed in the power of God and he was the closest thing to it on earth. He had the answers they so desperately sought. He was beside himself with joy.

All these things and more he was quite prepared to do. Why, he'd forgotten how downright deadly he could be. He hadn't used his talents in years. The rust was vanishing and the shine emerging. The rush of the alcohol was a Godsend. He began a relaxed walk around the room, reminding himself of the power he wielded. It was all just too easy. He'd begin by calling the blade first thing in the morning. But first he'd take another spin around town.

Little Frankie Spinelli was bored out of his mind. His aunts, uncles and cousins, all girls, were sitting around after Sunday dinner, and he'd had enough. A few hundred yards away was the field. He had his glove and his nearly new baseball and nothing to do. He was the man of the hour when he showed up with that. It was just the shot the kids needed. Besides, with a new ball he could be on Mike's side and pick his position. Maybe there'd be another fight. So he pointed himself toward the field and began walking.

Big Jim Carty loved Sunday dinner. There was nothing quite like gathering around a table of hungry Irish and listening to them gab their way to the bottom of their plates about the old days in the old country. The malarkey ranged from dull to unforgettable depending on the story teller. The more people the better the chance of a fantastically told lie. With a talented gabber present, the house would fill magically, the Guinness would flow and good Irish Times would be had by all. Whether the tales were true or not was another thing. No one gave a hoot if it was fact or fiction so long as it held your attention and made you laugh. What mattered was the telling. The story couldn't be serious though, or boring or who lost who in the Rebellion. The Church was out unless it involved humorous revenge on a nun who had it coming.

Criticism hindered digestion and ended the evening early. The critical had nothing to offer but a two hour headache with their volume of viciousness. He'd suffered through a meal with Pat Mac years before. To be sure, if you were absent you'd be the topic of their conversation. Thankfully none of his kind was at the table.

The get together had ended early for Jim. Perhaps there was an unforgettable tale or perhaps not. His mind was elsewhere. Nevertheless he'd thanked his hosts, made his excuses, and was the first to leave. Had his wife been alive she'd have insisted he sit and be still despite the tone at the table. Or his own.

Regardless of his tone, not so good at the moment, he drove to Tom's house, parked the truck in front and walked up the driveway. He battled back tears as he lit a cigarette under the arch of grapevine. He walked around the spacious back yard, to the discolored patch of lawn, where decades before Tom had them all over on a chilly Saturday morning chopping up a tree, root and all, downed in a hurricane. But happy he was to put his back into it with his mates, and later pile into a car bound for Dwyer's Tavern. There'd be bowls of stew and pints of Guinness. But only after every inch of that bloody tree had vanished from the ground, and the hole filled and seeded. Tom would leave nothing for later.

He shuddered at the memory of his wife and his friends, nearly all of them gone. He spent more time in front of the telly seeing only the dangerous days of his youth, or regretting this and regretting that. He sighed aloud and fought off the poison of his thoughts.

What never left his mind however, even for a day in fifty years, was the beautiful young girl, the love of his life, now long dead.

He was only twenty, walking back from church a million Sundays ago. He'd passed her on his way to church and was struck. She'd grown into a woman overnight.

"Why Jim Carty, aren't you the bold one. And what are you starin' at?" said Kate Kelly, a girl of exceptional beauty.

She was tall and smiling with black hair and hazel eyes and didn't care a bit about it. If she was four by four she'd have worn the same wide smile. Just happy to be alive and Irish. She was in the middle of three brothers and three sisters.

"Bold, am I, Kate Kelly?" walking a step closer and smiling.

Kate blushed.

"You're in the front garden watering flowers for County Cork to see, and I'm the bold one?"

"It's not a crime," she spat back. "As if I was tending me garden without a stitch on me back."

" 'tis a crime, the water you're giving 'em. And the answer to your question is foolishness. That's what I'm starin' at. On my way to church you were at it. Since then I've suffered for me sins, the Lord Himself promising me fame and fortune, I've said hello and goodbye to a dozen people, and you're at it still. You'll drown 'em with all the water. If you don't come to your senses now, they'll be dead by midweek."

She took a step closer. "A liar, you are."

He stepped closer. "Am I, now? How's that?"

"You've got flowers of your own. Why stare at mine? That's how it is. And they won't be dyin' anytime soon. They're flowers for Pete sake. They're made for water and sun." She rolled her hazel eyes skyward. "They told me so themselves, Mister Carty. And you still haven't answered me question."

He took a step closer. She took a step back. The front yard was a sea of color. A lattice of grape vines arched the front entrance from the dirt road. But her smiling hazel eyes and black hair were the only colors he saw.

"I'd tell ya what I was starin' at but you won't like it a bit, Miss Kelly."

"Uh huh. And you've the nerve to tell me, I suppose. Mister Carty."

Ooh, that stung. He'd succeeded brilliantly to talk himself between the rock of knowing what to say, and the hard place of tying his tongue into knots, and there he fell in love.

He could only widen his eyes, shut his yap, stuff his hands in his pockets, and feel as stupid as a mick could. The next few seconds of silence was eternity.

"I thought so," Kate snickered, emptying the water from the can.

"I, well, I..."

"Well, I have things to do, Mister Carty. And sure, you must have a barrel of important things, as well, seeing as you're bound for fame and fortune."

And with that kick in the crotch she started for the back of the house.

"I'll tell ya what though, Kate. Ah, I..."

But she'd vanished among the colors.

Well, it certainly wasn't his wit, or his courage in the face of beauty that got him a second chance with Kate. All week he'd cursed himself for his choice of conversation with her. He may as well have called her a moron, as if she knew nothing at all about the care of flowers. He'd watered his own every day since.

On his way to church the next Sunday he passed her house slowly. The flowers had been watered. They were tall, delicate and perfectly happy to be rooted where they were, swaying this way and that to the soft morning breeze. He must have only just missed her.

In church he traded favors with the Almighty, fame and fortune for one more conversation with Kate along, of course, with the right bloody thing to say this time. Throughout the service he stood, knelt or sat at the wrong time.

After church he spoke to no one. With his heart he practiced his lines, but his head began to manufacture the danger signs of total failure. She was avoiding him. Who would blame her? He had rocks in his head and marbles in his mouth.

The walk past her house was painful. He imagined Kate with someone else, someone who said all the right things, knew the names of all the flowers, when to water them and... Oh, well, he'd live somehow, but the image of her hazel eyes and her smile put an ache into his heart. Jim passed by her house and walked slowly home.

They seemed to come from nowhere. "Halt! Put your fucking hands in the air. Back the fuck up. And don't move a muscle or I'll blow the top of your head off," a voice with a British accent yelled. There were six of them.

"I've no weapons," said Jim.

"Shut your hole. Where were you? Give me papers."

Another grabbed the papers from Jim's pocket.

"Keep your fucking eyes to the ground," one yelled and frisked him for weapons.

The rest had their weapons pointed.

"What are ya looking for?" asked Jim.

"Open your filthy mouth again without being told and pay the price," said the same voice.

"I've just come from church. I've no weapons," said Jim stupidly.

From behind came a blow to the kidneys and from the front a rifle butt to the forehead. Jim dropped like a stone.

"Must be hard of hearing as well as stupid," another said.

He looked at the papers then threw them in the dirt. The soldiers walked away laughing and muttering

"They'll never learn. He'll wish he stayed in church. Church, did he say? There's no God in Ireland."

He awoke some hours later on a bed in a strange room. He tried to get up but the rush of pain to his head was too much. He moaned loudly and fell back.

Into the room came talking people.

"Jimmy. Lie still, lad."

"Bastards."

"Are ya all right?"

"We've some broth for ya."

Surrounding him were three men and Kate Kelly. She was crying and laughing at the same time. Laughing from relief that he'd come around.

"Jimmy, does it hurt much," she asked patting his brown curls.

"What do you think? Of course it hurts him," said a voice.

"Look at the size of the welt, would ya," said another.

"Hello, lads."

Jim looked at Kate and smiled.

"I'm here to tell ya, the Lord works in strange ways. So be careful what ya pray for. This is the chance ya take these days for tellin' a beautiful woman she's doing a grand job in her garden. I wanted only to tell you that, Kate."

"But you didn't and you should've. I watered 'em twice, waitin' for ya. " Kate cried and laughed.

"I'd have tied me tongue all up. Seems I put things plainer with me brains rattled. You've a splendid garden, Kate."

"Jazuz, will ya listen to him. A regular Willie Yeats we've got in bed here," said a smiling Tom O'Bannion.

"Is that you, Tom?"

"'Tis Jimmie. The bastards walked by my house laughing. I figured there was misery in their wake so I went to see, and sure enough. I carried you here. Kate took care of the rest. Can you see all right?"

Two weeks later there was a knock on Jim's front door. Tom O'Bannion and another man stood there. Jim scanned the area and then invited them in.

"Don't worry. They're miles away," said Tom.

"Jimmie, this is Sean Kelly."

"Are you the one drivin' me sister mad?" said Sean.

Jim smiled and shook the man's hand. "It's the other way 'round, I confess. I'm proud to meet ya, Sean. And I'm proud to have met yer da when I was a boy."

Kate had three brothers. Sean, the youngest, was IRA to his dying day and not a man to cross with steely black eyes and an unsmiling face. Kevin, the father, a man of the same look and temperament, was shot dead on the first day of the Easter Rebellion. Sean's two older brothers went to prison.

Within an hour of his father's burial he kissed his mother goodbye, rode east into the action and stayed for four years. He killed British and did it well.

Under British rule Ireland was a tortured landscape. Horrendous living and labor conditions, suppressive laws and taxes, poverty, human misery and hopelessness were the lot of the people. Worse than this even were the arrogant justifications offered by the bully, England. As if anything not British was without a soul and needed to be ruled.

In the year nineteen and nineteen the IRA was formed. Its intentions were complete independence and it wasn't kidding. It didn't talk or negotiate. It matched British ruthlessness with a passion. Its goal was a free Ireland, its purpose was to kill British. Any act aimed at damaging England or its sympathizers was regarded as patriotic.

"We're planning the social event of the season. A get-together with your old friends." Tom pointed to Jim's head. "Are ya up to it?"

Jim smiled.

The first act was a raid on a police barracks to get guns and ammunition. The police were Irish, not British, so there was no killing. Tom O'Bannion and Jim Carty were two of nine young men that night led by Sean Kelly.

It was a simple matter of knocking on the door to gain entry. In minutes they'd roused the policemen from their beds and relieved them of guns and ammunition.

Sean thanked them for their generosity then delivered stern warnings; they'd be shot the next time one of their own suffered at the hands of the police. Due to his height Jim stood out like a lighthouse.

The second act occurred twelve miles away only hours later. Kelley and his crew ambushed a British patrol on their way back to their barracks killing eight. The IRA then melted into the night.

In simultaneous raids the Brits sought revenge. Two nights later one British unit of eight men surrounded Kelley's mother's house, where only Kate and her mother slept. Miles away, in a not-so-safe house, were seven of the IRA raiders. Two sentries were posted outside, one with a stolen automatic weapon in a hilly field behind the house, the other across the road hidden among the trees, leaving Kelly, Carty, O'Bannion and two others inside.

The second British unit of sixteen men had motored their way to within a half mile of the house and took to the hills to come in from both front and back, in effect surrounding the place. One of the Brits coming from the front turned an ankle and yelped, alerting the sentry who ran quietly to warn the machine gunner. He then ran to the house rousing the five others giving them a precious minute to mount a defense or to flee.

The machine gunner, keeping to his position and hidden well, heard the squad of Brits advancing from his rear and within seconds had them in his sights. He waited until he could hear them breathing and opened fire. All eight men went down, dead or dying. He lifted his weapon to run to the aid of his mates but was shot in the back by a wounded Brit.

At the sound of the firing the eight Brits in front, not realizing soon enough their counterparts had been neutralized, began firing willy-nilly into windows and doors killing one man. They were surprised by Kelly and company, now outside and firing from both sides of the house. The first British unit was now caught in crossfire. One went down. But another Irishman was dead as well.

"Where the fuck are the others?" one Brit yelled. It looked as though the game was up when Jim and another man took bullets and retreated back inside. The crossfire advantage was suddenly gone. Of the four IRA trapped in the house, two were wounded.

Outside were seven healthy Brits. It was not looks of confidence the remaining Irishmen inside exchanged.

"I'm going for that machine gun," said Tom "We're done if I don't. Whatever you do, don't let them get around back."

With that he was gone. The remaining four then opened fire hoping to pin the Brits to their positions.

Tom made it the fifty yards to the gun. He circled the rocky field in back toward the front. The seven Brits then charged the front. Tom opened fire and three fell. The four remaining screamed their way inside and started shooting. The cries of wounded on both sides filled the night.

Inside was one dead IRA and one dead Brit. Kelly and Carty, both now wounded and out of ammunition, had surrendered to the three Brits.

"These two we need alive," said a powerfully built British officer holding a gun to Sean Kelly's head. "You two go and get that gunner. And find out about the others."

The squad who'd ravaged the Kelly home was now motoring their way to join their counterparts at the safe house. Without a word of warning the bastards had sprayed the house of Sean Kelly with bullets killing the only occupants, Kate Kelly and her mother.

The officer holding the gun spoke.

"Your mother and sister are dead, Kelly. And you're in for a painfully long night yourself."

Both men wailed aloud.

He then turned to Jim. "I'm sorry, have we met?" He punched the bullet wound in Jim's thigh viscously and whipped the gun across his face.

"Pardon my manners, you must be Mr. Carty."

Jim cried out, mostly from the news of his dead Kate.

At that there was gunfire outside.

"That'll be your late gunner. A lot of my men are dead tonight. You scum will be tortured as soon as the rest arrive. I'm gonna nail you to the floor by your own skin and then burn you both until I get what I want. And isn't it too bad about your dear old mum and sister. My condol..."

Tom crashed through firing. In a heartbeat the faces of Jim and Sean were covered in blood and brains. The Brit's head was nearly gone from his shoulders. Screams of terror filled the room.

"Let's go, lads. Sean, grab a side of him. I heard a motor in the distance. I think more are on the way. We've no time," said Tom.

"You're right. There's more on the way," said Sean.

Jim moaned loudly as they rushed him from the house and over the bodies of dead soldiers, two of whom were those sent after Tom only minutes before.

Safely atop the hill behind the house Sean spoke through tears.

"Jimmy, I'm sorry about Kate and all of this. And me own poor mum. Imagine those bastards. You two get going. I'll hold 'em off long as I can."

"Are you mad? The place'll be crawling with 'em any minute now," said Tom.

"Don't worry about me. I'll get a dozen more with that machine gun," said Sean.

"I'm goin' back with you, Sean," said Jim.

"Don't, Jimmy, please. Not in your state. I should've known they'd find the house."

Sean smiled and hugged both men. "Ah, Jimmy, it's a broken thing. It's all broken."

"Fuck them bastards, Sean. We'll kill what's coming our way, and we'll say our farewells to Ireland," said Jim through his own flow of tears.

"He's right, Jimmy," said Tom. "There's nothing left. They know who we are for sure. There'll be hell to pay now. There's too many dead Brits here. And four of our own. We've got to go, Jimmy."

"Get to Dublin, lads. See you soon for a pint. How's that? Now get going. It's an order."

With that a tearful Sean was gone.

The vision of Kate faded into the afternoon sunlight. How he missed his wife and the company of his old friend. By only their presence both were of a temperament to soothe, no matter the storms in his soul. A lucky man he was to have had both in his life. How was it they were gone and he was not? Punishment for the lives he'd taken those many years ago? No, that was war and they were British. His days he knew were numbered. What lay ahead after that was anybody's guess. How he longed for a good fight to know he was alive.

"Oh, Tom, how we miss ya today. I'm in need of a..." he snickered through his grief. "I'm in need of a bloody hole to dig, or a wall to build. Ah Jazuz, what the hell do I know, what it is I need. Tell us what to do Tommy, would ya. A heart attack it is maybe. Look at me, talking to meself out loud. And worse, I don't care who sees or hears. They'd expect that of an old mick I suppose. Me Margaret's gone for good, had enough of me is my guess, so it's you who'll be listening, like it or not."

Already the property had the look of a ghost ship. Never had he known any part of it to go neglected. The sight of it was breaking his heart. Was it two weeks yet Tom was gone?

Frankie parked himself at third hoping for a miracle in the form of kids materializing from the ether, all chatter and noise, not knowing or caring where they had come from or why they were there, busily choosing sides for a game. A robin dropped in for a snack, that was it. A little while later he sent up a quickie to Saint Francis but got no cooperation. Everyone was probably at their grandmother's for dinner or something. He climbed up third base because he'd never done it before. It was either that or go home.

What could possibly happen now? he thought, on his way to the field. Mr K had come in the front door with his bag of sauce and headed for the bathroom. Mike was in the cellar, heard it all, and bolted from the house. One day of school left. No more homework, no more books, no more of the Blade's insane rages. It lifted his spirits to know she'd be out of his life forever. Altar boy lessons had fizzled, praise the Lord for that. He'd only gone to two. His father had looked at the Latin text one night for a moment, grimaced sourly, began to yawn and then popped himself a beer.

Summer lay ahead where all kinds of adventure awaited. *Jeez, where in the world have I been?* he thought. All he had to do now was outmaneuver his father but that was light work. A few beers usually did the trick.

His usual stunt was giving nickels to his sisters to feed him beers. No matter what daddy was doing, if one of daddy's little girls brought daddy a beer they'd get a pat on the head and another nickel. Soon daddy would be out cold in front of the tube. Mike could then march boldly out the front door, glove in hand, and proceed to tear up the free world. His mother could bitch and moan until the shingles fell off the fucking house. And those left inside were welcome to listen.

Yeah? So what could possibly happen now?

Chapter 24

He didn't expect to see a soul and he was right. He walked over to first, looked around for a sign of the little deer, took a leak, and got that shitty 'nobody to play with' feeling. Then a voice.

"Miiiike Kilgaaaaalen," Frankie yelled slowly. He was nearly at the top of the tree, completely hidden by leaves. He cupped his hands around his mouth to disguise his voice.

Mike looked around stupidly.

It was beautiful. "Miiikkkeeee, over heeeere."

"Who? Where? Who is it?" Mike was completely baffled.

"Ooooverrr heeeere."

"Where?" Mike turned and turned with a big grin.

"Are you a Howdy Doody fan, young fella?"

"Come on, will ya? Yeah, I never miss a show." Mike was going crazy trying to solve the voice.

"Miiikkkeeee."

"Cut the shit, where are ya? Who is it?"

"I'm the ghost of center field. And you must answer."

"For what?"

"For ahm... taking a piss just now."

"Are you God?"

"Noooooo, he's my unkuuuulll."

"Then tell your uncle it wasn't me."

"He's not iiiiinnnn."

"Where is he?" Mike laughed.

"How the fuck should I knowwwww."

Frankie was laughing his balls of, literally. The nearly new ball, and the old black taped ball, which had been fouled off by Denis days before, tumbled out of his glove, banged off some branches, thumped to the ground, and gave him away.

"Frankie, you idiot," Mike laughed seeing the balls on the ground. "That was pissa. I never woulda found ya. You can't tell where the voice is coming from. It was great. Come on down." The glove dropped from above.

"What are we gonna do?" asked an invisible Frankie.

"Who knows? Seen anybody?"

"Nope," Frankie answered as he shinnied down third base.

Mike handed him his glove and ball.

"That was fucking great, Frankie," Mike said laughing.

"Thanks. Where is everybody?"

"Who knows," Mike said with a sigh.

"Hey, I know. We can play with sixteen imaginary men."

"Or! We could go swimming at the Johnson's pool," said Mike with huge inviting eyes.

Frankie recalled the hungry German Shepherd and the crazy gardener, and declined politely.

"Anybody home at Joey's?" Frankie lived a couple of houses from Joey.

"I didn't look. We could throw tomatoes at cars."

"There's none big enough yet," said Mike sadly.

"Where's the slingshot?" asked Frankie.

"Oh, yeah!" said Mike with a devilish grin. "Over behind the dugout. Pissa, let's go to my grandfather's."

"Why?"

"I don't know yet. We gotta go the long way, though. My old man's home."

The priest was cruising the parish in his usual 'defender of the flock' guise. It was not beyond him to knock on a door and inquire how 'little so and so' was doing in school or in little league or in life. It's how he developed most of his clientele. Nearly always a fatherless family, the surprised and thankful mother would welcome him humbly, serve coffee and allow the priest the run of the house.

That meant bedrooms and boys. In such homes there was always need for spiritual counseling of some sort and the priest was only too happy to offer his services. After a dozen dry runs the drill was down cold. He knew the easy marks, and he knew the ones to avoid.

Early in his priesthood he'd coveted a young boy for months to the point where his perverted compulsions led him one evening to the front door of the boy's home. The mother had answered his knock and welcomed him inside. The first minute went well enough. He'd mumbled a feeble excuse for his presence. Then the boy appeared and stood beside his mother, smiling at the priest. Shortly his demeanor had alarmed the woman to the point of calling her husband from upstairs. He then found himself staring at unsmiling faces, unable to satisfy anyone that the visit was anything but awkward and suspicious. He learned quickly to be prepared.

With his trusty prayer book in hand he'd enter the room of a boy and shortly have his way. They were vulnerable, silent and terrified. There was challenge, danger and satisfaction with every encounter. This was always the case. With satanic fulfillment his corruption of innocence continued unopposed. His tally of wounded souls was now innumerable. Mortal wounds never to be spoken of or understood, wounds which festered and multiplied, which never healed. He was a virus beyond detection, an ambulant plague that neither smiled nor frowned at the mounting death toll.

Jim had managed not to make a complete fool of himself, either to himself or his departed friends. He hopped into his truck and headed out. He'd expected a call by now about the contents of the greenhouse, storehouse and the cellar, and what should be done with Tom's tools and equipment. But he'd heard not a word from anyone. Maybe he'd head over to Brian Reardon's house and ask him. But how the hell would he know? If he knew anything he'd have called. If anyone would know it'd be Tom's daughter Claire. He felt in no mood for them but it was no time to be thinking of himself. If he was the one in the ground Tom would've seen that his tools were properly cared for. It'd be a nice gesture to pay a visit and offer his services if needed. Maybe he'd see Mike in the bargain.

Whoever said Nature abhors a vacuum knew his stuff. Yes indeedy. It's a theoretical and practical fact of life. Sit for a spell and do nothing. Look at a wall or a book. Pick something and watch it, don't move and above all don't think. Got the idea? Now, observe as those idle moments soon dwindle into a free for all of mental goulash. Then, let's face it, it's either find stuff to do, or go get into trouble.

Mike and Frankie chose both, due in large measure to the fact they didn't want to go home to two big idiots who were doing exactly what they were doing, but long ago had forgotten they were doing it. Something to think about.

With a wicked accurate slingshot they parked themselves, like snipers in the dirt, under one of the Late Tom O'Bannion's thick fir trees and began taking pot shots through the fir at anything on wheels. But being good Catholic kids they aimed only for the hubcaps. At first.

Enough driving around, the priest decided. It was time to bring out the big guns. A little diplomacy and a lot of Authority might be just the thing. And what the hell, the poor woman could probably use some fresh air and sunshine. 'Sounds like a plan to me. Should do the trick' somebody in his head said. He'd apply as much pressure as he possibly could without killing the kid. The kid would get the message soon enough. The father would beat him senseless. A serious visit from the boys and girls in black would be enough to stop any heart mid-beat. *'Don't forget to bring up the electric chair and what devils do to little boys in hell. Get's 'em every time,'* another voice insisted. Hand over that bloody photo or die slowly. Yeah, he'd get the message okay. He headed for the convent.

F̲ive minutes into their assault on a peaceful society on a quiet Sunday afternoon, they scored a direct hit on a shiny metal hubcap. The guy jammed on his brakes which scared the hell out of the kids, thinking for sure they'd been spotted. He was out of the car so fast they didn't dare make a run for it. They could only sweat it out.

"Jesus! What the hell was that?" he said to his wife as he walked around the car.

The kids could only see from the guy's knees down.

"Scared the hell of me," said the wife from inside.

"Me, too," the guy said. "It sounded like a bullet, fakrisake."

The kids watched from the dirt without batting an eye. If the Red Sox had marched by in formation, neither kid would have noticed.

Then the guy closed his door and squatted for a closer look at the side of the car. From front to back he scanned every inch for a new scar and some satisfaction. His wife joined him shortly. The kids saw high heels, stockings and the bottom of her dress. He stopped at the hubcap and felt the heavy gauge metal with his fingertips.

"What was it?" asked the wife as the guy continued.

"I don't know, scared the hell out of me though."

"Me too. I thought something had exploded."

Then the guy leaned over so his eyes were nearly to the ground and looked precisely where the kids were lying. "Whatever it was it seemed to come from right there."

Mike was about to come out with his hands up because he thought the guy was pointing right at him, actually speaking to him. The guy kept blinking into the blackness right at him. Mike was sure the guy heard the pounding in his chest.

"Is there any damage, Harry?" the wife asked.

"I didn't see anything," said Harry still staring in. Then he looked up and scanned the length of the trees. "Son of a bitch, what the hell was it?" Harry said as he got back behind the wheel and slowly drove away.

"Oh, my God," the little bastards whispered as they finally relaxed.

"That was too close," said Mike. "We can't use rocks anymore."

"No more rocks," Frankie agreed with great relief. "That guy looked right into my eyes, Mike. And he didn't even see me. I almost shit my pants."

"No more rocks," laughed Mike.

"What can we use?" asked Frankie.

"Let's go see what's in the greenhouse."

Jim pulled up in front of the Kilgallen house and made his way up the front walk. He felt like he was doing the right thing. It seemed the neighborly thing to do. After all, Tom and he went back more than half a century. Surely they'd understand that. Well, bing-bong, here I am.

"Oh, my God," said Frankie. The two kids stared into the basket like two hikers who'd stumbled across a neatly wrapped pallet of hundred dollar bills in the back woods of Maine.

"Will they squish?"

"Let's see," said Mike. He picked a reddish one from the top of the pile and placed it into the webbing of the slingshot. Gently he drew back on the web, the rubber stretched and the strawberry squished. "Shit," he said, tight lipped.

"I'll hold it," said Frankie, taking it in both hands. One on the handle, one straddling the prongs. "Try it now." Frankie held it out stiff armed and took his position.

Then an idea. Mike took the strawberry out. "I know." He pulled the web back, then he inserted the strawberry. It fit snugly between the two rubber bands and nearly into the web.

"Okay, hold on." He drew back and let it fly. Like a lightening bolt it shot across the length of the barn to the big front double doors and struck with a wicked sounding 'fawop'. It echoed briefly.

"Oh, my God.' they both laughed.

"Grab a side," said Mike. Out the door and across the lawn they ran with a bushel basket of strawberries.

Meanwhile, back at the convent, the Blade was spending her Sunday afternoon in much the same fashion she had for forty years. Well, not quite. The regular school year had her hopping. Sixty three children were taught six subjects daily then assigned lessons to do at home. At a minimum that was a few hundred pieces of paper to collect daily, and then grade. Five days a week, four weeks per month for nine months, minus a few vacation days. That added up in more ways than one.

She would welcome the summer. The year was coming to a close and all the final exams were in and being graded, and there she sat doing her best to crunch numbers in every students favor, even the trouble makers and the very dull. There was a soft rap on her door as she tapped her pencil thinking of one particular student.

"Mike, try a practice shot on that."

Frankie pointed to a green Ford parked almost directly in front of them across the street. Through the perfect camouflage of fir they had clear side to side vision measuring two feet by about five inches high. More than enough. They could see where the front quarter panel met the door, down to the tail light and from the ground up to the door handle.

"Good idea," said Mike.

He loaded up and let it fly but it disintegrated in mid flight.

"How come it worked back there?" asked Frankie.

"Hold it tight, Frankie."

"I can't hold it any tighter."

"Give it to me. Let me try something." Mike wedged the handle between two small branches, one on top of the other, about three inches apart. He drew the web back from the prongs. Perfect. He now had a rigid base, good as concrete.

"Give me a strawberry."

He drew the web back and inserted the strawberry between the two taught strips of rubber, as close to the webbing as possible. It was a perfectly snug fit.

"Here goes."

At the speed of light it smashed into the passenger door of the green Ford.

"Unbelievable," laughed Frankie.

"Frankie, load me up."

Mike drew back the rubber, Frankie gently placed a ripe one between the taught rubber strips and tapped Mike on the head, like a couple of Marines at the Battle of Okinawa.

"Three, two, one..." It hit with a thud like a watery bolt, a foot to the right of the first one.

"It's better than a ray gun," Frankie said in awe.

No God-fearing passerby noticing strawberry juice on the bottom half of the car door would've ever imagined how it got there. The great Inspector Holmes himself would have been helpless, seeing only thick branches of fir brushing the sidewalk, waving slightly in a gentle breeze.

"Quick, here comes a car."

Mike drew back, Frankie fed it a strawberry and tapped Mike's head. The car caught it on the rear door with a nice dull thud. It slowed but it didn't stop. They laughed and laughed. The next one got it behind the headlight. They laughed some more.

"Strawberry invaders arrive on Earth!" Mike laughed as he popped one into his mouth.

"The great strawberry invasion!" Frankie added, popping one in his mouth.

"What if they were cantaloupes?" Mike smiled.

"Oh, God," laughed Frankie.

Between breaks in the action they worked on the green Ford. It was a dream come true for two kids with a little bit of the devil in 'em and nothing to do on a Sunday afternoon.

Draw-load-tap. "One strawberry? Coming right up, sir?"

WWWWAAAAPP – explosion on impact.

Driver – "Christ Almighty Jesus!"

Car slows.

Driver – "What the hell was that d'ya think?"

The kids roar silent laughter. Car drives away.

Draw-load-tap. "Something in strawberry, sir?"

RRROOOMMF – direct hit, driver door.

Driver – "Jesus H. You hear that?!"

Car slows.

Driver – "Did you hear something just now?"

Wife – "I think so."

Car drives slowly away.

Kids laugh themselves silly.

Draw-load-tap. "Do we have strawberries? Do we ever."

PINNNG – bulls eye, hubcap.

Driver – "Holy shit! What was that?"

Car slows.

Driver – "Did we just hit something?"

Guy gets out, looks around, then drives away.

Tears of laughter.

Draw-load-tap. "Did someone say strawberry?"

THRRRRAAAAKKK – front quarter panel.

Driver – "Mother of God. What was that?"

Car slows down.

Wife – "Don't get out, they might be colored."

Between moving targets they murdered the green Ford. What was now strawberry syrup, from a hundred hits, had dripped down the side and was baking in the sun.

Draw-load-tap. "Strawberry paint? Why yes sir, I believe it does come in strawberry." WWWAAAPPPP.

"A little darker up front?" he nodded to Frankie "I think my associate and I can handle that." FFFFRRR-RUUUPPP.

"I'm afraid not, madam," Mike smiled "It only comes in strawberry." WWWWAAAAKKK.

"Strawberry windows? We don't do that here." WWWAAAAKK

"Strawberry hubcaps? Why the fuck not, lady." BBBRRAPP

"Strawberry tires? Doctor Spinelli?"

"Why the fuck not." TTTHHHUUMP.

So many strawberries — so little time. They'd killed the better part of the afternoon and were just about to pack it in when the silence was broken with the sound of ticking. It came from their left and it gave them both pause. Whatever it was, it was too slow for an unwary motorist, much too slow. The ticking came from an engine. An engine which seemed to have a purpose, as if waiting for a scent, certain it was in the right place, growing louder as the seconds passed, and more ominous. Not unlike the ticking of a grandfather clock in a spooky house at midnight. There was only the ticking, like a deadly mechanical predator sniffing out something to eat alive. Mike smelled the exhaust fumes, unaware of his hand squeezing the dirt beneath him. The daylight seemed to evaporate around them. Hair on their necks and arms came to attention. Slowly it approached their tiny field of vision, slower than slow, too slow not to be something other than a grave threat. The ticking turned to thunder, matching their heart-beats. It was black, and it took forever to blot out the green Ford.

The Blade and the priest were in the drawing room off to the right of the convent's entrance. The priest was pleading his case about crucifying Mike. Of course, he'd mentioned a couple of other names in the bargain so as not to arouse any suspicion.

Isn't it a terrible state of affairs? Parents taking no responsibility for their children's education. Leaving it all to the poor suffering nuns as if they had nothing else in the world to do. Isn't it, after all, a two way street? Couldn't they at least lend a hand with the homework assignments instead of soaking themselves in Seagram's and beer in front of Sid Caesar night after night? How about a little help folks, for heaven sake! An example had to be set, someone must be made accountable.

"Let's face it Sister, we have our limits. We can't do it all ourselves. I'm not saying these things to dampen your spirits, but I for one would like to see a little justice. We cannot be sending these children into the world ignorant of consequences. In my hands are the transcripts of several such students. Ah, here's a perfect example, Michael Kilgallen."

It was working. He could see her face tighten as she nodded in agreement.

"Two years worth I'm holding and this just isn't satisfactory. Not even close. You have a heart of gold, Sister, but look at the markings he's received in conduct and religion, not to mention the rest. Deplorable! Why, I ask myself, is he even taking up space at St. Catherine's. Have you an answer for that, Sister? Have you?"

Jim sat on the sofa with his hat in his hand, not feeling quite right about it all, especially after his minor tiff with Mr. K the day of Tom's death. Nevertheless, here he was, waiting for the kettle to whistle, while Mrs. K rustled up a snack to go along with tea. He'd offered a mild protest but she'd insisted. He only wanted to help with Tom's estate, wanting nothing for himself. But as yet he'd not gotten the chance to bring this up. There were formalities to suffer. At least Mr. K, somewhere around the house, and probably not too happy at all about Jim's presence, hadn't tossed him out.

The color from their faces drained and their breathing stopped. The words BOSTON POLICE rolled into their line of vision between the branches of the fir, words written in white block letters on the side of the ticking black car. They heard the squawk of the radio and muffled cop talk.

"This is it. Right?" said one cop.

"Big fir trees. Across from fifty-five. Kid's throwing apples or something," said the driver.

"No pumpkins, though," said the other with a laugh.

Frankie was on the verge of tears. Mike put his shaking hand on Frankie's shaking arm for comfort.

"See anything?" asked the driver.

"Hold on."

The cop on the passenger side opened the door and his black shoes hit the street. He walked the few feet to the trees and began his search. The kids could hear the cop separating branches for a look see. He was now coming their way, and the driver's left elbow was inches from the green Ford which now resembled a frozen strawberry daiquiri. No genius IQ was needed to connect those dots, thought Mike.

"Give it a quick look underneath and let's get going," said the driver.

The priest and The Blade rounded the corner and pulled up in front of Jim's truck. If ever there was a sight to take the breath from a set of ten-year-old lungs this was it. This was judgment day, report card day, final exam day, the end of the world as we now know it, all rolled into one neat little black package on wheels. The two Authority figures strode purposefully up the walk, up the steps, to the door bell.

'Gee, who could this be?' thought Mr. K, farting around the basement workbench holding his fifth frosty of the day.

The more sober Mrs. K didn't like the sound of the bell. Something she didn't like traveled with it. A seriousness, someone perhaps whose duty it was to be there. She counted the whereabouts of all four. The girls were in the back yard, the baby beside her, but Mike was, as usual, God knew where. Regardless, she swallowed nervously and licked her lips. It was Sunday afternoon in late spring with storm door ajar, real world separated by the screen door. Anyone they knew would've yelled something and just walked in. She squashed back her apprehension and headed for the door.

Jim heard it, rolled his eyes, and regretted showing up on a Sunday. He'd be in the way of family or something else and this was all beginning to fizzle.

The cop had gone the length of the tree line bending and looking. It was a full minute before he arrived. The shoes were two feet in front of them, dull and scuffed.

He took a frustrated breath, "Ah, Christ," he said huffing and puffing, "how do you toss apples from this stuff? Makes no sense. Think about it. Where're the apples? Nothing on the street."

Frankie couldn't take another second and started to flee. Mike grabbed his shirt as the cop bent for a last look. The kids were flattened into the dirt.

"Come on, forget about it. Let's go get coffee."

"Talked me into it. Nothing but bugs, anyway."

The cop got back into the ticking black car and off it went. Mike and Frankie started to breathe again.

After a minute Mike spoke. "Let's get out of here. Help me bring this back."

Inside the barn they couldn't speak for awhile. They were shaking like leaves.

"Frankie, next time I say something like, let's go swimming at the Johnson's pool, let's go swimming at the Johnson's pool. Okay?"

"Next time."

"We gotta get out of here," Mike said, looking out a window. "Right, now."

Then Frankie burst out laughing. "I wonder what that green Ford looks like."

"Not too green anymore. There's a million strawberries stuck to it. My arm's killing me. Half the basket's gone. Come on."

"Oh, my God. What if the cop lifted up the branch? Oh, my God. Oh, my God."

Mike sighed deeply. "That was too close. We gotta go. Come on."

"What about this?" asked Frankie holding up the slingshot.

"Leave the slingshot. Take the glove."

Chapter 25

At the top of the driveway behind the house Mike gave instructions.

"Stay here. I'll walk down to see if the coast is clear. If it is I'll signal. Count to twenty, slow. Then start walking but take the long way to your house. Don't follow me, go the long way. Got it?"

"Yeah."

"See you at the field, okay?"

"Yeah."

"Bring your ball. Don't forget, okay?"

"Okay."

Mike got the bottom of the driveway, looked around, gave the all clear, and disappeared from view. Frankie began counting, slowly, behind a tree, with his eyes closed.

At the count of five the owner of the green Ford and his new bride walked out their front door.

At twenty Frankie opened his eyes and began walking gingerly down the driveway, actually expecting to see cops on the roof, in the trees, zooming up the driveway with pistols and shotguns drawn.

The smiling new bride rounded the front of the car to the street. At that precise instant Frankie walked out of the driveway, onto the sidewalk, no more than ten feet from the woman.

"Oh my God!" she exclaimed, backing away.

The husband looked up at her, and also noticed Frankie. He walked around to her side. Half the entire side was layered in a rich strawberry syrup. Frankie looked at them, they looked at Frankie. Frankie panicked and began to sprint the short way home.

"Hey, you! Kid! Hey!" the guy yelled.

But Frankie was running for all he was worth and then some.

"Honey, call the cops." Then he screamed, "Oh, my God. Look at my car, will ya."

Mike took the long way. Home was a straight ten minute shot from his grandfather's but he took the most round about path he could think of, killing a good half hour. The encounter with the cops was close, but the further he walked the more relieved he felt. He could only imagine arriving home in the back of a cop car. He'd be tied to the pipes in the cellar and beaten hourly, fed with a long stick once a day for the whole summer. It'd be lights out no baseball, no sunlight, no contact with another human.

His thoughts gradually lightened, however. He and Frankie had dodged capture and arrest. School was nearly over, the field would be a mob scene of picking sides and playing baseball all day long. Dinner would be ready shortly. He took another big sigh of relief at the thought of narrow escape. Oh brother, if that cop had come a foot clo...

This is the police. You are surrounded, come out with your hands up. Michael John Kilgallen you have been duly convicted and sentenced to death, to be carried out forthwith. Do have you any last words?

His tongue dried up and his legs went soft. He saw electric chairs, a scaffold with a guy under the noose holding a prayer book, a guy in a hood holding a huge axe, standing beside a block of wood. Waiting. The world before his eyes had turned dark, threatening, and treacherous, not unlike the dinosaur world of Albert's books. He was surrounded by giant meat eaters.

In front of his house sat Jim's pickup and the priest's black car. A Boston Police car was parked across the street, passenger side tires on the sidewalk a couple of feet from the neighbor's stone wall. Somehow the cops had found out. Another chill went through him. How? They'd found out, that's all that mattered. Frankie, at least, was safe. But he was a dead man.

The shock of his upcoming execution eased only enough for a short bit of analyzing. The priest was there for obvious reasons. The cops as well. Jim? Who knew? But he was glad Jim was there. His parents would be sitting like a couple of parrots listening to Authority weave a woeful tale about the state of his soul and his future criminal career. It was pointless out-waiting them. Get it over with. So Mike slowly made his way around the corner, eyes glued to his front door.

Rounding the corner he spotted something odd inside the cop car. A lump he could not discern. It moved. He hid behind a tree and watched it. It moved again. He ran to where the hedge began and crawled the length of it until he was at the car window. The same hedge he'd used to spy during the priest's last visit. In the back seat was Frankie.

Mike crawled under the hedges to the sidewalk and rapped on the glass. Frankie popped into view, his eyes red from crying.

Mike opened the door and whispered. "Frankie, what happened? Never mind. Just get out and follow me. Now, Frankie, now!"

Frankie was moving too slowly, nearly out on his feet from fear. Mike had seen it in school after The Blade had beaten some kid half to death.

"Give me the glove. Follow me. Be quiet."

Frankie squeezed out the door and followed Mike under the hedge, onto the lawn. They crawled to the end of the hedge, out of view of Mike's front windows.

"Frankie, do they know your name?"

Frankie broke into tears. "They didn't ask my name. They only wanted to know what we were firing at the cars. The guy who owned the green Ford saw me and called the cops. Mike, I told them who you were. They were gonna send me to reform school if I didn't."

"So they don't know your name?"

Frankie shook his head. Mike handed him his glove.

"Get going, Frankie. Don't stop running 'til you get home, okay?"

"Okay." Still sobbing he trotted across the street and into the field and started running. Avoiding the front of his house Mike headed for his secret hiding place behind his neighbor's garage.

Inside the house were cops, clergy, terrified parents, and Jim, still looking out of place. His mother sobbed every time anyone spoke, his father rubbed his knees and chain smoked. Both resembled defendants awaiting a jury's return. Mike, it appeared, was headed for the big house or the hot house depending on who had the floor.

Mike emptied his bag in the grass. He sighed nervously at the sight of it, and the mission ahead. He needed an envelope for the photo. He'd slip it to Jim somehow, and hope for the best. He sent up a quick Hail Mary to his grandfather, and promised whoever was listening that he'd do better in school next year.

Half-way through the prayer he heard an alarming and familiar sound. He waited and heard it again. It was Frankie's panicked voice screaming wildly from the woods near the field. He quickly filled the bag, put it back on the shelf, and made the sprint across back yards, road and field, to the edge of the woods.

The cries came from where they'd had the fight with Gary and Creature. He tip-toed past some bushes for a closer look. Frankie was on the ground. Gary, Creature's brother, towered above the terrified kid, wearing the same get-up as the day of the fight, heavy engineer boots and all. He held a knife. Mike picked a nice juicy rock from the ground, held it at the ready and made his way further in.

"Hey, Gary! You fucking bully. Why don't you pick on somebody your own size for once," said Mike.

He picked another rock from the ground.

"Well, if it ain't Davy Crockett, king of the wild frontier." Gary seemed too sure of himself. "We came looking for you a little while ago."

"You and Casper the Friendly Ghost?" said Mike seeing only Gary.

He cocked his throwing arm.

"Frankie, get up."

Gary quickly dropped to his knees and put the knife close to Frankie's face.

"Drop the rocks or the kid gets it. I ain't kiddin, and no, asshole, not me and Casper. Me and him."

Gary pointed behind Mike.

Coming across the field from the direction of Mike's back yard was another freak in engineer boots with an evil grin on his face. He was thick in the chest and arms, had short wiry hair and looked as though he enjoyed inflicting pain.

"They caught me, Mike," said Frankie.

"What are you gonna do with the knife?" asked Mike.

"You'll see, asshole. First you gotta meet Otto. Otto just got out of jail. We're celebrating." He moved the knife closer to Frankie's face. "I said drop the fuckin' rocks."

Mike dropped the rocks. Gary stood and lit a Lucky Strike.

Otto arrived carrying a paper bag. Mike's paper bag. From his secret hiding place. His eyes opened wide in fear. Otto was one of the creeps that had taken over the field the summer before, and tossed all the gloves into the stream next to first base.

"Remember me?" said Otto, stopping in front of Mike.

He held the bag up, smiled and punched Mike in the stomach with all his might. He walked over to Gary while rummaging the bag.

"We got us a camera. Might be worth something."

Mike rolled on the ground trying to get a breath.

"Nice. That yours, asshole?" said Gary. Mike rolled in the dirt sucking wind. "This his?" he asked Frankie.

"I don't know. I guess so," said Frankie, sobbing. Still Mike rolled, struggling to breathe.

"Where'd you get it, asshole?" said Gary.

"He emptied his piggy bank, like little faggots do," offered Otto.

While sucking wind Mike had a frightening realization. If his courage betrayed him here he was truly fucked. If that photo disappeared he was a dead man in more ways than one. So... he squeezed out a reply between gasps of breath.

"I stole it down the Square, zit-face."

"Why you little fucking bandit," laughed Otto. "You go away for that shit."

"If you're dumb enough to get caught, you fucking idiot," said Mike.

Otto balled his hands into fists and laughed out loud. He turned to Gary with an admiring grin. "I'm gonna enjoy the shit out of this."

"Here's the thing, asshole," said Gary. "I got a knife. You got nothing. We got yuz both and we're gonna fuck yuz both up. For this."

He lifted his shirt revealing a half-healed slingshot wound on his back.

"I figure I take a piece of your ears, your noses, too. One for me, one for my brother."

"Yeah. Wherever the fuck he is. He's missing a great party," added Otto.

Frankie's sobs intensified as he imagined life with no nose. He'd been nabbed by the two thugs as he headed home, through the woods. At knifepoint he'd pointed out Mike's house to his captors.

Otto had walked across the back yards and spotted Mike, on his knees behind the garage, busy with a paper bag. He'd seen Mike react to Frankie's cries, fill the bag, hide it, and then run to the field.

A shaken-up Mike finally got his breath and stood.

"Let him go. He's only eight, you chicken shits."

"Ooo-ooh," snickered Otto.

"Chicken shit, huh?" Gary moved to Mike with the knife held out.

"That's what I said, pizza-face, and that ain't all I stole down the Square, either," Mike said, hoping it would pause Gary. It did.

"What do you want? A fuckin' medal? So what."

"I got a watch, some rings, and a pile of money. And I'm going back for more. It was easy."

Gary and Otto were all ears now. "I don't fuckin' believe you, kid. I say ya lyin'."

"Oh, yeah? Zit-face." Mike yanked the pile of cash from his back pocket.

Gary and Otto nearly came to attention. Mike backed up a step, and began his fiction. "Army-Navy store across from the Fairmount Theatre. Simple. The old guy can hardly walk, never saw me."

If these two were as stupid as they looked they'd be locked up by Monday night. Mike would warn the guy himself. The two bullies would be gone for the whole summer.

"I got a compass, too. Get up, Frankie. He walks away. I drop the money on the ground. It's a hundred bucks."

He saw the surprise on the faces of the two bullies.

"Give us the money first," said Otto.

"Yeah, right," Mike snickered.

"I'll cut the kid wide open."

"And I call the cops."

"The one's in the trees?" laughed Gary. "I said drop the money."

"The cops at my house, asshole. It's my uncle. Tell the stupid Nazi to walk over and see. His cop car's right out front. Go look."

Otto did, and was back in a flash, huffing and puffing. "There's cops all over the place. Let's get out of here. Now, Gary."

"Let him go, or I start screaming for my uncle, Captain Kilgallen. Wanna go to jail today, asshole?" Mike then eyed Otto. "It's Otto. Right?"

Gary now had the lost foggy look of a gambler who'd bet his roll on a straight flush, only to be beaten by a higher one. His rapid blinking told the story.

"Get out of here, shithead," he said to Frankie.

Without a word Frankie grabbed his glove and ball, and was off and running once again. Gary pointed the knife at Mike. "I'm gonna get you one of these days, asshole," he said to Mike. "Now drop the fuckin' money."

"We don't need this shit. We'll get him later," said Otto, rubbing his hands.

Confidence soaring, he ignored Gary's threats. "Put all my stuff back in the bag, pizza-face, and put it over there. Or I start screaming. I bet my uncle, Captain

Kilgallen knows all about Otto. Right Otto?" Mike gave Otto a nod and a smile.

Neither one of the bullies moved. Mike called their bluff and screamed. "HEEEEELP!!! Dad! Uncle Phil!

Suddenly Otto was happy to comply with Mike's wish. In seconds the bag of goods was on the ground exactly where Mike had intended. The thugs began a slow retreat.

"I'm gonna fuckin' get you," said Gary.

Mike picked up his bag. "Fuck you pizza-face. It's my money." He dropped a dollar on the ground and said, "Get some Clearasil, Gary."

With that he ran from the woods to face his next challenge.

He walked in through the front door. The Masters of the Universe were in his living room this Sunday afternoon. And Jim, still looking a bit out of place.

"Ah, here's my boy now, the nation's most wanted criminal. Come in son, have a seat and tell us all about your day."

This was said with threatening sarcasm. His mother dropped her head into her hands and once again began to sob.

"It was strawberries. I did it, everything. All alone. What a blast. Good afternoon, Sister."

His mother sobbed even louder, his father bared his teeth.

"Well, young fella," one of the cops said, "we're glad you had a good time. You boys could've caused some serious injury. Do you know that? And I'm sorry to say we have your sidekick in the back seat out there with a different story to tell. We're on our way to his house, right after we wrap up this half," he said, smiling knowingly.

"Oh. Okay. Want a beer, Dad? Jim? Officers? Sister?"

Seven pair of eyes opened wide in shock.

"Sit down in that chair you, and wipe off that smirk. There's a priest and a nun in this house. And if you didn't notice the police are here. Now, you tell us what it is you've been doing the whole day. From the last time we saw you until this very minute, kiddo. Or I swear..."

Mike saw the slight grin on the priest, ignored his father's command and walked over to Jim. In his hand he held the neatly folded paper bag which contained the incriminating photo of the priest.

"Jim, this letter is from my grandfather to you. It's real important. I was supposed to bring it down to you on my way to school but I forgot. I put it in my secret hiding place with my bottle money and forgot. I'm really sorry," his eyes pleading for Jim's understanding.

Jim accepted the note, mesmerized. The kid was running the whole show.

"He wanted you to have it right away. He said it was really, really, really important."

Jim got the drift, sensing something of a dire nature. Curious, he began unraveling the bag. He stood and walked to the hall.

"Christ, on a side car!" he mumbled quietly, his back to the rest. He turned, walked to Mike, and shook his hand.

"Your grandfather was a hell of a man. A courageous man. You'll stop down for a coke soon, will ya, Mike. I'll tell ye a story."

"Okay."

"This is what I came to pester you for Claire. You'll never know the relief the note means."

He sent a glance to the priest and chuckled.

"Wait'll Tom's friends see this. Won't they be surprised. My thanks for the tea and a good evening to you. You'll stop by for that coke, Mike."

And with that he was on his way.

"Strawberries for God sake," he laughed on his way out the door.

The priest now wore the worried expression of a man who'd just received the worst possible news from his doctor.

The remaining six adults were by now reduced to players on Mike's tiny stage, reduced to supporting roles in they knew not what.

"Excuse me, Mrs. Kilgallen. I'll be right back," said one of the cops "I'd like to remind your son of something." Within seconds he was back. "Son of a..." he stopped himself, "kid's gone."

The other cop rushed out the door. "Mr. Kilgallen" said the cop rushing after his partner "you have a ten year old kid that may one day become a menace to society if something isn't done to, to, to put him in line. I'm letting this go because no damage was done. But be warned."

And he was gone. Outside the two cops looked up and down and all around, then got in the car and drove away.

Mike took out his Groucho glasses, put them on and smiled at the priest. The Blade nearly had a fucking stroke,

"Well, I never in my life, Mrs. Kilgallen, have seen the like of it. Never, I tell you. Father, you were absolutely correct about this boy. He's possessed. It's something from a devilish nightmare. If you please, Father." She stood to leave.

"And you," she turned to Mike "oh ho, ho ho! I'll be looking forward to another year with you. Oh, yes. It is going to be some fun. If I were you I'd be praying that Sister Beatrice Serene is called by the Lord before the seventh of September."

"Yes, Sister," said Mike.

The parents hadn't moved a muscle, figuring perhaps the kid had lost his marbles in a fall from a tree or something. Mrs. K searched her son's head for bruises and swelling. Mr. K could only watch and wonder. They were looking more and more like numb skull characters in a Laurel and Hardy episode, hardly believing the crazy scene taking place before their eyes.

"And you, father?" Mike asked "A high-ball? We have shit-loads."

The priest sat, clenching and unclenching his jaw. The color in his face had vanished.

"Mary Mother of God! It's him! In this house! The anti-Christ!" the Blade screamed, "Father, let us be gone from this place."

"Because," Mike continued, "you're gonna need a shit-load."

Chapter 26

The very next morning Duckpin and Snake, showed up at the rectory. With warrants. The first was to search the premises. The second was the arrest warrant. They would use both no matter what. They were real curious because the kid in the picture that Jim brought down to the station was the spitting image of the kid they had in custody the day before. But they were wildly enthused to introduce themselves to the priest, and see for themselves his resemblance to the figure in the photo.

They rang the bell at ten minutes before nine on Monday morning. Father McAuley answered. They flashed badges and warrants and he moved out of the way. Three more cops followed them and soon the rectory looked more like a murder scene than a rectory. Poor Father McAuley swallowed hard and stood still.

"Where is he? Devlin, where is he?" said Duckpin.

From the second floor near the top of the stairs they heard it. Laughter.

"What's all the hullabaloo-hoo-hoo?"

At the top of the stairs was a shock and a half.

"Your late, you silly policemen, all of you, late as all get out. I've been ready and waiting for hours."

Down the steps he strode in high heels and a girdle with garter belts hanging loosely, and swinging with each step. The blue robe was open. His nails were polished red, as was the lipstick. A pink scarf was wrapped once and hung to his waist. It was all topped off with long blonde hair. He held a drink in one hand and a cigarette with holder, in the other.

"Call the men in white coats," said Duckpin from the side of his mouth.

"You have got to be shitting me," said Father McAuley, handing Snake the phone.

The priest sashayed from the bottom of the staircase over to the fireplace in the living room. All eyes followed, perhaps afraid at first to do anything but watch.

"The heels are from Paris, they're all the rage, you know. I think the archbishop will adore them. Don't you? Can I get you something from the bar, officers? After all, it's way past five."

He sipped his drink and puffed a cigarette while shifting positions. The others could only watch, stunned.

"I suppose you're here for the truth, the whole truth and nothing but? Well, you've come to the wrong place. There's no such thing. I should know. Oh, yes indeedy I do. The boys? Those boys, you understand... Well, let me tell you... Are you sure you won't join me?" He held up his glass.

"Sit him down, officer. In the other room. Cover him up. Cuff him. Gag him," Duckpin ordered one of the cops.

Snake came back. "They're on their way."

"Holy shit," said Duckpin "You think you've seen it all in twenty years on the job. Then this," he swallowed hard.

One of the officers came down from upstairs. "Sir, wait'll you get a load of his bedroom."

Duckpin only nodded and rolled his eyes.

The moment the priest was placed into the ambulance by the men in white coats the Blade was passing out final exam reports, desk to desk. The final day of school would end at noon. The young faces were as happy as could be. Despite her own upcoming vacation her day had begun badly. The all too familiar nightmare had lasted too long this time. She'd not slept well and the headache was back. This minute the Bells of St. Mary's were pounding away behind her eyes.

Yesterday, she'd visited the devil himself. The little monster, who had the nerve to show up and take his seat like an evil apparition, wasn't helping.

Lately her thoughts of dying were consuming more of her day than at any time previous. She'd be sorely missed and wouldn't the world grieve, miss her dearly, and all she'd done to make grand little soldiers for the Lord's work here on earth. Loved and sorely missed by thousands, she'd be.

Presently she was walked the aisles. The usual routine would be to have a student or two see to it but the end of the school was hours away and she welcomed the distraction. It was very warm even with all the windows opened. She sweated buckets under several layers of wool garments. She thought bitterly that perhaps none of these little devils would ever appreciate her hard work and selfless sacrifice for their well being. And their parents as well, now probably getting the family ready for beaches and playgrounds and ball fields with their hot dogs and pretzels and beer.

The major portion of her life, nearly forty years as a teaching nun and how many visits from past pupils? Two? Three, maybe. Letters? Not a single one. How many times had a former student crossed the street in avoidance upon recognizing her. Too many. Did they think she was stupid? Didn't notice? Couldn't they see that the pain they had endured at her hands was for their own good? No. Emphatically no. It was a burden she'd carried for too long.

She approached Mike's desk and stood a moment, glaring. Mike sat unafraid, completely calm, unshaken by her presence. She barely contained an irresistible impulse to grab him by the hair of his arrogant little head. She did however slam the results of his tests hard onto the desk.

"See you in September, Mr. Kilgallen."

She turned to continue, lost her footing and nearly fell to the ground. Tommy Cassidy froze in his seat. It was his foot she'd tripped over.

"I, I, I'm-m-m-m s-s-ssorry sis-sis-sis... The Blade grabbed Tommy by the hair and began her brutal routine. Everybody froze in their seats.

"You did it on purpose. I know you did," she screamed.

Mike rose from his seat, lifted his desk, took out his freshly sharpened number two pencil and slammed the desk top loudly.

"Leave him alone you big fat fucking pig. Leave him alone!"

He cocked his fist high in the air and let fly. The point found its mark in a roll of ass blubber. The Blade straightened as if she'd been electrocuted, eyes wide in shock. Mike then kicked her as hard as he could.

The student body gasped and went stiff.

She reached around and pulled out the pencil.

"Ah, ah, ah. Oh, Jesus in heaven."

The Blade limped from the aisle. Mike had gotten clear.

"Brenda, run for Sister Agnes Gertrude. Do it quickly, dear."

Brenda ran like a cheetah down the aisle and out the door.

"You. You! I've been waiting for this day to dawn. Today is the beginning of your hell on earth. Your last day at St. Catherine's. You'll be in reform school before the end of the week, like a common juvenile delinquent."

She held the pencil high.

Mike stood with his eyes as wide as they could open with his mouth tightly closed, his breathing rapid.

"Taken by the police, from this school, away from your parents and put before a judge."

Her face was a mix of shock, pain, rage and revenge.

Tommy was crying. Mike ran to Tommy's desk.

"Come on, Tommy. We're leaving. Let's go. Don't worry."

"Thomas Cassidy, you sit right back down in your seat, this instant," the Blade screamed.

The entire class was as still as an ice sculpture.

Mike and Tommy raced through the cloakroom, to the steps, and made their mad dash out the front door, down the steps, to the street. Soon they were far enough away to walk easily but kept looking over their shoulders.

They walked for many minutes before either one spoke. Tommy had not taken his eyes from the ground.

"Mike, w-w-what's gonna happen?" Tommy managed.

"Nothin'."

"How do you know?"

"I got a feeling, I guess. That's all."

But they both looked worried, and it was some time before Mike spoke.

"You like rockets, Tommy?"

"Yeah, I guess. Why?"

"My friend's making one."

"Oh, yeah?"

Mike told Tommy about Ray and how smart he was and all the stuff he knew, and Joey's school, where nobody got beat up. That seemed to cheer Tommy up.

"Wanna get some ice cream?"

"I guess so. Okay."

"Let's go to the joke shop first. They have really neat stuff. Then we'll get some ice cream. Okay?"

"Yeah." Tommy turned to Mike and smiled.

"Then later we'll go to my friend Ray's house. He might need help with the rocket."

"How big?"

"Wicked big. Did you see, Day the Earth Stood Still?"

Mike and Tommy wore wide smiles. This was better than great baseball, beating up Creature and Gary, and all the fun he ever had with his friends combined. He'd be expelled, he'd get his ass kicked, and God only knew how he would explain things to Mrs. Cassidy. But at the moment he couldn't wipe the grin away. His secret was vanishing, and seemed to have not the slightest importance to him. It would never be known by another and, though he didn't know it yet, no boy would ever again suffer at the hands of the priest.

Mike and Tommy crossed the bridge, into the Square.

"Say hey, Mike."

"Hi, Willie."

"Do me a favor, would ya?"

"Yeah sure," said Mike.

"Sign my glove?"

"Yeah sure. Coming to the field later?"

"You know that. Don't eat too much ice cream. Might slow you down," said Willie.

"I won't. Can ya bring some guys?"

"It's done, Mike."

"And a ball, too. Okay?"

"And some peanuts and crackerjacks, too. See ya at the field, Mike."

"See ya, Willie."

The End

INFALLIBLE

ABOUT THE AUTHOR

Brian Dillon was born and raised in Boston, enduring nine years in Catholic grammar school with the Sisters of the Guillotine. He went on happily and enthusiastically to attend public high school somewhere in Boston. He joined the Marine Corps and did his bit deep in the jungles of Viet Nam.

His favorite action hero is Ben Franklin.

His wish is that more Americans would read, understand and apply the Constitution of the United States in the manner in which it was intended by Our Founding Fathers.